DATE DUE

Help us Rate this book...
Put your initials on the
Left side and your rating
on the right side.
1 = Didn't care for
2 = It was O.K.
3 = It was <u>great</u>

———————————— 1 2 3
———————————— 1 2 3
———————————— 1 2 3
———————————— 1 2 3
———————————— 1 2 3
———————————— 1 2 3
———————————— 1 2 3
———————————— 1 2 3
———————————— 1 2 3
———————————— 1 2 3
———————————— 1 2 3
———————————— 1 2 3
———————————— 1 2 3
———————————— 1 2 3

SECOND EDITION

"*The Shade Tree Choir* is the story of a boy growing up in a dysfunctional family. The family disease of alcoholism affects six and a half million children. Having alcoholic parents increases the chances that a child will become an alcoholic between five and seven times. Dry statistics are easy to ignore but David Nelson gives a face and a heart to the child growing up in that environment, and shows the reader the real pain that the disease can cause. He also gives us insight into factors that can moderate some of the damage--- teachers, friends, and their parents play a significant role in keeping the young character Krame from going too far down a dark road."

"Those looking for a good read will find this to be a well-written and engaging novel. For those looking for hope, however, *The Shade Tree Choir* makes the case that fate's choice for parents need not condemn a child to a lifetime of misery."

Dr. Frank Wagner, Professor of Behavioral Science
University of Medicine & Health Sciences, St. Kitts

Shade Tree
Choir

David Nelson

SECOND EDITION

Dedicated to...

... my wife Jean, my best friend, who has seen the best and the worst of me, and yet we are still in love;

 to my brother Richard (Rick), who was with me in the trenches during our childhood;

to my sister Margaret (Maggie), who has been for me an unfailing source of love and support;

to my astute and sensitive editor, Gretchen Houser. She has been the exemplar of editor values;

to Carl Short, for his guidance, technical support, and mentoring. I shall forever be indebted for his calm demeanor;

to Tom Schweikert, my best childhood friend, who gave me friendship and kindness and refuge;

to Dave, Becky, Bryan and Rich, for all the good times;

and to all survivors of alcoholic parents, dysfunctional families, and child abuse.

"May the worst day of your futures be better
than the best days of your past."

Irish proverb

Table of Contents

Apologies Before the Fact

Boys, especially inner city boys, frequently resort to cussing, and in particular, have a tendency of dropping the F-bomb whenever and wherever possible. The story behind *The Shade Tree Choir* is no different. Whether it was an inability on our part to come up with a better word, or a showing off to our friends, or simply a way to feel powerful, the word, in all its derivations, was common usage at the time this story took place. My apologies if it offends.

Prologue

I struggled for air and could only whimper for him to stop hurting me. I could feel my ribs being crushed against the floor by his heavy weight on my upper back. The sheer force of his hand stung my wrist as he pulled my arm behind my back and yanked sharply upward. I thought he was going to break it off. The shag carpet ground against my face like sandpaper and I could feel the tearing of my skin. My nose pushed into the fibers and I could barely breathe through the burning sensation of pain. I gagged at the smell of the filthy tattered carpet, at the stench of a decade's worth of dog waste and urine. As I struggled weakly against his grip, I choked on the odor of unwashed feet, mud, grime, and ground-in food. My stomach heaved at the sickly scent of bourbon and beer and hopelessly, my tears and sweat mingled into the carpet beneath me.

Why was my dad doing this awful thing to me? What had I done to deserve such treatment?

I was eight years old.

Chapter One: The Death

The tires of the plane hitting the runway and shuddering along the ground brought me back to reality. As we taxied to the tiny terminal, I saw my older brother, Mark staring out the terminal window, waiting my arrival. Of all my six brothers and sisters, he was the only one I kept in contact with since leaving the area eighteen years ago.

"How was your flight?" he asked, clapping me on the shoulder.

I took a deep breath. "No problem; just too long. How are you doing?"

Mark shrugged, scratched his head. "Oh, okay, about as well as could be expected. God, I can't believe how he died. He never ever told me he loved me. Before he passed he regained consciousness, sat straight up and called me a son of a bitch! Then fell back down and died," he said disgustedly. "God, nice memory I'll have forever, huh?"

"Yeah, he was a tough son of a bitch, all the way to the end." I picked up my suitcase and we started walking. "Is everyone here? How's Mom?"

Mark grimaced. "She's fine, you know Mom. You're the last to arrive. The wake starts in another two hours so I thought we'd go right to the funeral home. Okay with you?"

"Yeah, sure," I said, but dreading it all the same. "That's fine."

Not much more was said on the ride to town. My stomach filled with acid and my legs felt weak as I climbed the steps of the funeral home. Opening the front door, the stillness and the pungent smell of flowers almost overcame me. My two younger brothers met me at the door and the mechanics of the hand-shaking ceremony saved me, gave me time to compose myself. I hadn't seen either of them in nearly fifteen years and we treated each other like neighbors, chatting about the flight and the weather, avoiding any mention of how we really felt. But then, none of us knew how to express feelings, true deep-down feelings. Dad had taught us well.

The sound of laughter and chatting greeted me as I walked down the hallway and entered the "viewing" room. My three sisters were there with their husbands, probably sharing a joke or gossip that was clearly funny. I gave each a hug and wondered how long it'd been since I last saw them. One thing hit me as strange. Nobody was crying, not one person, In fact, most people were standing around talking, eating, and laughing. Dad would have said, "Ha, ha, very funny," in his deep-throated, gravelly voice, now silenced forever.

"Hi, honey," Mom said as I turned toward the casket.

I gave her a half-hearted squeeze and asked how she was doing. "Oh, fine. As good as one could expect, I suppose. Do you want to look at Dad?"

"Yes," I replied, knees shaking. I wondered if he might rise up out of the casket to hit me one final time. This guy was the toughest person I had ever known.

His nails were trimmed like he was some type of white-collar worker; the cuticles cleaned and waxed. The hands, however, were atrophied to the point where his metacarpals were visible, sticking out like sore thumbs. The serene look on his face was unnatural and out of character. Since he rarely dressed in anything other than a checkered shirt and solid pants, I guessed the dark brown three-piece suit was borrowed. His hair was combed! I never remembered my Dad's hair being combed; that's why he was given the name "Bushy" at his job. The funeral director said he looked natural and I thought the funeral director was full of shit.

Gone were the bruised and battered knuckles and the oil and dirt stains filling the wrinkles on his hands from years of work as a machinist or trying to fix the stubborn family car that rarely worked. The once-powerful hands, which held many a sharp switch or belt to beat us, were nowhere to be seen. The black raspy stubbles on his cheeks were missing and replaced with a pinkish rouge.

But why not? At age 53, after fighting cancer for three years, Bushy was dead. Some considered me as the black sheep and others considered me an outsider. I considered myself a rebel and a survivor, and was proud of it.

I never learned to let others into my deep inner circle or to share feelings. Bushy taught me that. He used to say that was how real men behaved. While I felt sad for him now, I felt no grief. I felt strong inside and showed no emotion. I don't remember one word the minister at St. Peter's Lutheran Church said that day. I was busy watching the reactions of my siblings. There were occasional sniffles from my older brother and sister, no reaction from me or my two younger brothers, and uncontrollable sobbing from my two younger sisters.

After a long, arduous trip across town to Linwood Cemetery and yet another service, we were finally headed back to my brother's house and through the neighborhood we had all left years before. Nothing was said in the car as we drove down Windsor Avenue. My mind felt vacant until the bells of Sacred Heart suddenly jarred me from my stupor just as we crossed the tracks at East 22nd Street. It took me back thirty years earlier when the bells would resonate and ring, but never crack, each hour of the day.

"Stop!" I demanded. "Pull over here!"

"What's wrong? What do you want?" Mark asked.

"I'm going to walk the old neighborhood. I need to be alone for a while."

"Are you nuts, you dumb ass? It's not safe here," he said as he pulled along the high curbing to let me out.

"I'll call you if I need a ride but I'll probably just walk back to your place," I said as I got out of the car. "And I certainly can take care of myself."

I scanned the corners and streets for signs of gangs, the tough guys who had replaced the innocence of kids a generation, now long gone. But I saw none. I removed my tie and stuck it in the inside pocket of my sport coat that I had thrown over my shoulder. I headed back up East 22nd Street and passed one house after another, run down houses that should have been condemned years ago. Screen doors hung on their hinges and pieces of plywood were nailed over the windows. Small strips of grass had been replaced with dirt, gutters leaned feet away from their rooflines, and one junk car after another littered the street.

We were all poor back in the 1950s in that neighborhood, but we didn't know it. We kept up what we had and no matter how tattered our clothes appeared, we were all clean when it mattered. And we protected our turf because we were proud to be from the North End, but no more, no more. This was a new place, a different place. And I thought, "God, what a pit."

Still numb and devoid of emotion, I lit a cigarette, turned, and there I was standing in front of a storefront brick building. I closed my eyes and listened, and heard the long ago sounds of children for a moment. Just for a moment. The building I was looking at used to be called Huey's.

Chapter Two: The Shade Tree Choir

In 1957, our territory on the North End of Dubuque was not a great expanse. Our roaming was bounded on the north by Windsor Avenue, by Rhomberg on the east, Kniest on the south, and East 22nd to the west. Movement beyond those limits was by express permission only. However, if an eight-year-old was daring enough, he could always sneak past the lines of motherly defense, brave the dangers of traffic, and find himself off the map, exploring the vastness beyond the Audubon School playground. If you got caught, the penalty was severe: we'd all felt the sting of a newly snapped and skinned lilac switch smartly applied to our tiny buttocks. But we had to face the danger; the threat of whizzing cars and the whistling of the switch is just too small a thing to dampen the wanderlust of young boys. And ours was a wanderlust sharpened and amplified by the knowledge that out there, beyond the pale, was an El Dorado worth risking it all to find: Kress's Confectionary.

Had we been able to search the world over, no cache of gold and silver could equal the treasures to be found in Kress's: Duncan yo-yos; black licorice, two for a penny; High Flier kites; hard penny candy; packs of Topp's baseball cards, five cents each; seven-ounce bottles of Coca-Cola and Bubble-Up; ice cream sodas for one fat quarter. So many delights that no amount of money or appetite could ever consume.

Kress's was located on the corner of East 22nd and Johnson Street. The children in the neighborhood called it Huey's, after the owner and operator, the man behind the counter whose life's work it was, it seemed, to stock every luxury a child could imagine. It wasn't until I was seven or so that I even realized Huey's store had another name, or that it offered bread, bologna, and milk along with gumdrops, malted milk balls and solid rubber baseballs that ached for the pulverizing swat of a junior Louisville slugger (and which would eventually be lost to the roof of Audubon, there to disintegrate in the sun and rain).

Huey's store was old. At least the building was old. On the outer wall a barely visible sign painted in red, white and blue advertised Wonder Bread ("Helps Build Strong Bodies in 8

Ways"). Years of bouncing rubber balls off the wall and catching them in the middle of Johnson Street had chipped most of the paint from the pitted bricks. However, the age of the building belied the newness of its riches.

On either side of the entryway, two dimly lighted cases exhibited the newest toys and comic books. Behind the glass cases, built-in wooden shelves from floor to ceiling housed a greater assortment of red wax lips, candy cigarettes, bubble gum cigars, jacks, pencils, notebooks, and binders. Directly opposite stood a marble-topped counter protecting the cold cavernous cylinders of genuine chocolate, strawberry, vanilla, and black raspberry flavored ice cream. While a ambulatory towhead was free to wander throughout the store (an excursion that could take anywhere from a minute to an hour), no one crossed the marble barrier except Huey. You'd pay your nickel, he'd go behind the counter, and roll a perfect ball of ice cream into the scoop and place it just so on top of a wafer cone. Two scoops went for seven cents.

Between the display cases and the frozen delights was an aisle; at least, that's what it should have been. Not in Huey's, however. That space of no more than ten by fifteen feet was occupied by a jungle of wire racks and baskets where tiny bodies could get lost examining the latest in genuine, imitation leather or miniature big league gloves—a buck twenty-five! —And balsa gliders (one fat quarter, and one skinny dime). Such was Huey's store, a small consumer paradise in the middle of a denying, abusive, oppressive parental inferno.

If a nickel could not be earned, the drainage ditch at the far south end of Audubon School almost always yielded a two-cent deposit pop bottle discarded by some extravagant teenager. Huey kept stacks of pop bottles in crates out back of his store, surrounded by a seven-foot wooden fence. It had a gate that was locked only at night from intruders in the alley. He only kept it latched during the day.

We never believed adults fully appreciated the essence of Huey's. How could they? They would rush in for a pack of Luckies ("L.S.M.F.T.") or a quart of Hilldale milk without ever stopping to scan the latest Tarzan comic book through a pair of colored cellophane 3-D glasses (fifteen cents).

Resting on the three-foot boundary wall of a neighbor across the street from Huey's, I finished my cigarette and wiped the limestone from my dress pants the best I could. It was in this very spot that Jim Clay's dad collapsed in a drunken stupor that summer of 1957. He left The Euchre Spot just across the street from Huey's, having swilled down boilermakers all afternoon. He could go no further and passed out. Having soiled himself, His pants reeked from the urine and shit that went all the way to his ankles. We continued throwing balls against the wall, trying not to get close to him. This was an everyday occurrence and we just ignored it.

And then . . . high above Audubon School, I saw it: the largest and most majestic elm tree in all of Dubuque County. It was a landmark to us kids, a *real* landmark. That tree represented the boundary zone between Huey's and the school. "Thank god, it's still here," I actually said aloud.

The upheaval of the root system had for generations provided a meeting place for kids. The roots were larger, closer to the tree and thinned out as the distance grew away from the massive structure. The best sitting positions proved to be against the larger roots projecting from the base of the trunk. These were saved for the older guys as a gesture of respect. No girl was ever allowed to occupy a seat. Ever! Now that was tradition. I sat at the base of the tree on the best root nature had to offer, and for a moment, thought I heard that song of some thirty years ago.

Our song was bellowed to the tune of the "Death March" -- "Poor ole Merle, for the worst is yet to come—Hey!" The "Hey!" was the most important. The more pissed we were from a beating, or lack of supper, or getting screamed at, the louder we went "Hey!" The subject of our ballad was Merle Niehouse. Mr. Niehouse (as we called him when we wanted to get into the school to get a drink of water or to have him fix something) was the janitor at Audubon. When we were safe at the edge of the playground, he was simply Merle.

We called it serenading. Adults called it disrespectful. Merle Niehouse called us assholes. He was the cellar monarch at Audubon. If a door needed fixing, a hinge oiled, or if a toilet was stopped up, he was the one to whom the teachers went. They would stand at the entrance to his sandstone-lined office, cup their hands around their mouths and yell for him. Nobody dared go down the darkened steps to the room where a one 60-watt light bulb burned over his small desk.

What better way to prove how tough we were than to sing to an adult who epitomized our fathers? So each time Merle would come out of his concrete sanctuary, we all began our chant of disrespect. He was a man in his 40s who commanded respect (but didn't get it from us) and instilled fear whenever we were within arms' reach. For it was at that distance we could smell his rancid tobacco breath, tinged with alcohol. His nose was a moonscape of pockmarks. When he bellowed down the hall for a six-year old to stop running, his deep, thunderous voice would rattle the windows of the 150-year-old structure. Then he would become even more cantankerous when he had to clean the shit from the floor the little one had dropped after being frightened.

Every time I saw him, he was wearing his olive khaki uniform. We all figured he wore green underwear to match the green ooze coating his teeth. His green ball cap was always twisted to the side. It sat high on his head, the brim tilted up in the air so he would have an unobstructed view of the little bastards provoking him from the elm tree. Poor Old Merle was an alcoholic like our fathers. He would just as soon swat us in the butts as to yell at us. All of this was allowed in schools in 1957.

He had a habit that entertained us to no end. Put short: he couldn't walk anywhere without scratching his balls. We would each imitate him and giggle after he had long passed. One day, right in front of Miss Egleholf, he stood there gnawing and pulling at his balls with one hand and plunging a finger of the other into his nose until the knuckle line stopped it. Miss Egleholf was a spinster schoolteacher whom I adored. She was strict, and she was fair. In spite of her rigid demeanor, I could tell she liked us kids. Her room was a safe haven for me.

So here was ball-scratching, finger-plunging Merle, standing there taking orders from Miss Egleholf to clean up the mess. Forty-five minutes earlier, Timmy Clipperfield had puked in the inkwell of his desk and splashed his chunk-filled fluid all over the floor, just missing the back of Rich Balkert. That chaos, way over in row one, was funny until the fumes reached me in row six. Then it was not so funny. For the next fifteen minutes I planned a state of war against the old fart for not coming quicker to our room with his sawdust, broom, and dust pail. However, it was difficult to concentrate with my eyes watering and my nose burning. That day after school we bellowed as loud as we could to the Death March. Merle never did come out. So the Shade Tree Choir had to wait another day for revenge—Hey!

Chapter Three: The Cigarette Caper

I don't remember how most of us met. I do remember my boyhood friends of so long ago, and I still can't believe that all except one are now dead. I realize now we were all part of a support system of survival for one another.

Many kids in the neighborhood were from large families of ten to fifteen children. All were poor, and nearly every father was an alcoholic, and even some mothers, mine included. My family consisted of seven children and was relatively small, but our distinction was simple; we were non-Catholic, while most of the families in town were Catholic. The church played a powerful role in all our lives. Our neighborhood was the largest and the poorest in the diocese. I found the Catholic Church useful for my private needs. I used to walk the streets looking in the gutter for large cigarette butts. Then I would go into the Church of the Sacred Heart and steal matches to light my newfound booty. The Catholic Church literally lit my fire.

Many of the fathers were veterans of World War II. Many abused alcohol. At one time Dubuque was second only to Munich, Germany, as the city with the highest consumption of beer in the world. The world, mind you! On nearly every major intersection there were at least two bars, with names such as Ten Pin Tap, Whitey's, The Sands, or the Euchre Spot. Maybe it was the influence of the church, the alcoholism, and the war. Who knows? Maybe it was John Wayne that shaped these families and individuals. But it's a fact that where I lived, alcohol use was prevalent.

Whatever it was, most of our fathers were of the old school that said there was no sharing, no crying, no questioning the establishment, and no touching (except with a belt, a board or a boot).

Sitting on the three-story fire escape of Audubon a few weeks after I shot the "bird" to Bobby Crutchfield, I was hiding, lonely and bored, looking for action, when I spotted Blackie Weinholter and asked him to join me. Blackie's real name was Orville. He was a wiry little kid with the nickname of Banshee. We only heard him called Orville when his mom was pissed and would beat him on the back with the two-inch leather strap that hung by the door, the weapon of his mother's choice that prevented Blackie's quick getaway.

I once saw him trip on the broken down, rotted porch as the screen door behind him slammed shut. He fell on his back and was caught by the morbidly obese woman who gave him life. His skin was in shreds and everywhere, there was blood. He twisted, crawled, and finally rolled onto the dirt below his family had the nerve to call their "yard". He jumped up and in a high-pitched voiced yelled, "Ma, you fuckin' *bitch*. I hate your guts!"

This was normal behavior. I just stood and waited for him to make his final escape from the torturous hands of his mother. "Orville" was always getting beat up by his mother—"Blackie," on the other hand, was my tough-talking, tough-headed friend. He was a kid of medium height for our mutual ages of eight years. His front tooth was chipped diagonally in half and shone like a pearl whenever his filthy face cracked a smile. Blackie reeked of fuel oil even in the summer when the heater was off. The stench must have been embedded deep into his skin because he always smelled of it. Broken, knotted laces that were too short to go through every eyelet held his tennis shoes together. The soles were held together with any kind of tape he could find and more often than not were in need of more adhesive. Even though Blackie was a fast runner, the condition of his shoes often got him caught as the rest of us sprinted to safety after ringing door bells and running down the street. We all liked Blackie and never gave a thought to his odor, his dress, or his lack of manners. The only ones who ridiculed him were the Sisters of Sacred Heart. To top it all off, Blackie was that rare thing in our neighborhood: the *only* child of a Catholic household.

Blackie was a daredevil who would often think of new escapades for us to try. He was out for blood against any adult and thought nothing of using the word 'fuck' with whoever was around. He hated the Sisters, he hated his mom, and he hated his position in life. If he didn't start a sentence with his favorite "f" word, there was surely one in the middle, and probably one at the end for good measure.

Blackie's mom was the most frightening woman I had ever known, then or now. She was huge, an obscenely fat, German woman. I guess her feet were too big for regular shoes so she went without, revealing streaks of dirt caked into her feet and long greenish toenails that had not been trimmed in years. She always wore a long housedress with deep pockets on each side. Her dress hung shapelessly over her 300-pound body, except at the arms where it pinched the wide, flabby globs of fat that swung back and forth as she waddled from one room to the other. She had black hair on her arms like a man and wide, fat fingers that could easily choke the life out of man or child. Her favorite term of endearment for Blackie and his dad was, "You no good, dirty, son of a bitch." She used that phrase a lot, flinging out those words like arrows, her face swollen with rage and pug nose flared, sucking in more fumes from the oil-fueled house; that horrible house that she never left.

When she was really pissed, the black hairs sprouting from the top of her nose stuck out like those on a wild boar. All this, combined with the rancid tobacco breath and brown teeth from years of smoking Pall Mall cigarettes, and her body odor of sweat, urine and fuel oil made *her* a no good, dirty, son of a bitch! She hurt my friend and that didn't sit right with me. A boy's heart shouldn't be filled with hate, especially about someone else's mother, but I couldn't help it. I doubt there was a boy alive anywhere who wouldn't feel the same.

The chrome kitchen table propped up her weight day after day as she sat there constantly smoking cigarettes and swatting flies. She was a non-practicing Catholic who would beat Blackie the minute he slipped with a "hell' or "damn" - which of course caused him to yell "Fuck!" the more she beat him. Then she'd force him to go to confession to repent his sins for cussing. He never actually went, but lied about that to her. And there it was, *another* sin piled on top of the first.

Blackie's dad never spoke. It was no wonder with a wife like that. He too was of German descent. He had not a hair on his head but made up for it on his chest and back. He looked like an ape and had strong powerful arms, hands, and shoulders. His rippled muscles filled the filthy tank top he always wore; the huge tattoo on his right shoulder and upper arm impressive to us eight-year-olds. We never asked what the anchor meant. We knew better. His strength came from years of working at the Dubuque Packing House or the "Pack" as everyone called it. He was a lugger and could single-handedly carry half a cow from the freezer to a refrigeration truck bound for far off places in America. Every night after work, his high-top, laced work boots predictably scuffed the ground as he walked the short distance to Whitey's Tap for a Star beer. He'd flick ashes from his Pall Mall cigarettes into the cuffs of his green pants as if this was a mannerly thing to do. We wondered if he bought his pants at the same place as Merle Niehouse.

The only time his clothes were changed was when he was totally drunk and soiled himself, in one form or another. His behavior was different from that of a normal drunk, something that happened every night in nearly every household under red or green roofs in my hometown. A normal drunk is when the fathers would simply pass out in a chair and get up the next morning to repeat the cycle anew. Once I was walking the railroad tracks, or "tracks" as we called them, and cringed at seeing Blackie's dad heading my way. He was on his way to work at the Pack and carried a black lunch pail in his right hand and held a Pall Mall in his left. I smelled alcohol, fuel oil, and vomit just a few feet away. I said hello, but he never spoke, only shot me a mean glare. I did notice his clean clothes for the day and thought to myself that he was totally drunk.

Us kids learned our life lessons early on. A rule of physical survival was never, ever enter into any friend's house far enough that you might get trapped by a parent on an alcoholic rampage or an older brother who might be pissed and beat the crap out of us. I'd broken this rule only once during my younger years. I learned early how to survive. I never had a friend sleep over for the night and, as was the custom whenever somebody wanted me to come out and play, they'd just stand outside and yell. That was the custom and my friends knew to never cross that line.

"Blackieeee," I yelled through the rotted picket fence.

"Get the hell out of here, you dirty no good son of a bitch," was the response from within as I heard the snap of a fly swatter.

"Blackieeee," I yelled again, knowing the tub of lard would never come out after me.

"Are you deaf? Get the hell . . . " Blackie piped up, letting me know he was on the way. He came rushing through the front door pulling his t-shirt over his head. He jumped off the porch in one big leap and in the process, kicked up some dust that swirled at his feet. He slammed the fence gate shut behind him. "What the fuck is up?"

I ran along beside him. "I stole two L&M cigarettes from the old lady's pack. Wanna go up to Audubon and light up?"

"One of these days she's gonna catch you,' he said, wagging his finger. "Then you'll be screwed."

"Naw. I'll never get caught 'cause I gave this lots of thought and figured every angle."

Blackie kicked at the sidewalk. "Yea, that's you, always thinkin' and always figurin'. Why don't ya just do it and worry later?"

"Because . . . you gotta figure every angle in life, otherwise you get caught. I swear, between my dad and your ma, one of us is gonna end up dead!"

"I'll tell you one thing," Blackie said, a worried look on his face. "If anybody comes around Audubon, I ain't sharing. You can, but I ain't. You got any matches?"

"Yeah, I went by Sacred Heart and stole some on the way over," I told him.

We headed for the playground. A few minutes later we were sitting against the trunk of the elm tree near the ballfield. We felt important, being as no older boys were around and we had the choir loft to ourselves. I gave him a full length L&M smoke and we both struck a stick match against our zippers to ignite.

Blackie burst into song. "Poor Ole Merle, for the Worst is Yet to Come—Hey!"

I inhaled, then exhaled. "What are ya doing? This is Saturday! The old bastard's probably sound asleep from last night. Heard there was some big euchre tournament at the Ten Pin last night."

"Oh yeah. I forgot what day it is," Blackie said, scratching his head. "So, how do you steal cigarettes without getting caught? This I'd like to hear so we don't have to walk the gutters anymore."

I explained my system. "This is so neat, and it's so damn easy. I tear off the stringer at the top of the package. Then I carefully slide the cellophane off the entire pack. Ya have to be real careful not to tear it 'cause ya need that later. I then take one of the old man's razor blades out of its holder and gently cut the bottom open to the pack. Ya cut the bottom of the pack open and take out two smokes from the center. It has to be the center so when it's all put back together it'll look full. Then I use a tiny piece of scotch tape and reseal the bottom, slide the cellophane back up, and there ya go."

"That is really good. What a great fuckin' idea," he said. "But what happens when your old lady sees one package's been messed with?"

"Oh, no problem. I open every single pack at the top when they buy a carton. That way they all look the same. They're both drunk anyway and don't pay any attention. If they're sober they just blame it on the factory. Been doin' this for a year now and never got close to being caught."

"Holy fuck!" Blackie exclaimed. "Can you imagine what the shit would happen if your old man walked in and caught ya?"

"Yeah, that's part of the excitement," I said, my voice getting louder. "My heart races faster and faster cause when ya start, ya can't quit. Ya have to be sure everybody is out of the house—old man, old lady, brothers and sisters. When it's all done, it makes the smoke taste even sweeter."

Blackie got all excited. "We could do that with Ma's Pall Malls 'cause they're a lot longer."

I shook my head, no, no. "Holy shit! Your old lady scares me more than my dad. Besides, your ma never goes anywhere."

Blackie was practically jumping up and down with his news. "I heard them talking about some cousin in town who died and they might go to the funeral. We could do this. I'll let ya know. Good for the heart, right, buddy?"

Later that day Blackie raced up to me and could barely talk, he was so out of breath. He had torn this tennis shoe again, running around the neighborhood looking for me.

"You won't fuckin' believe this! They are both going to the funeral at three o'clock today! And guess what? She has a full carton! This will be the best day ever!"

We made a plan. We'd sit on the cement structure supporting the railroad signal across the street from Blackie's house, and wait for them to leave. I had never, ever been inside the dilapidated, two-story house. I actually never went past the outside gate. We waited, and finally their car pulled out of the driveway. Blackie's parents drove past us with a dirty look we could feel through the closed windows. It looked like his ma was mouthing something about "bitch."

We waited a few minutes and when the coast was clear, we approached his house. A broken wooden door was lying on the porch that I stepped over, realizing that was what had tripped Blackie a few days earlier when his ma caught him and used the belt. By the time I opened the torn screen door, he already had nine packs of Pall Malls laid out on the table along with scotch tape and a rusty razor blade.

"Where's the tenth pack?" I asked. "Don't ya have a new blade?"

"Naw, the old man just had this one. Ma took a new pack with her to the funeral home."

"Just be real careful with the blade. There can't be any tears in the pack," I commanded.

After I showed him how it was done on the first two packs, he continued with the others. I looked around for a second escape door but there was none. I did notice the linoleum was torn in several places, exposing the wood floor beneath. Four wooden chairs surrounded the small red and white metal table. The cast iron sink behind one of the chairs had a torn curtain on the bottom I guessed, to hide things. On the opposite wall was a metal cabinet covered in scratches, chipped paint and grime that looked like dried boogers. A closet was used as a pantry; that was where she kept her smokes. Next to the closet was a fly swatter hung on a nail, and next to that was the leather strap.

I couldn't help but notice a picture of Jesus hanging on a wall with rosary beads decorating its frame. I wiped my sweaty face with my arm and told Blackie I had to piss. He pointed down the hall as he worked feverishly on his project. The grit on the floor felt like sandpaper as I cautiously walked the darkened hallway. There was no door on the bathroom. I wondered if that was the one on the porch. I stepped one foot in and about passed out—Jesus Christ, doesn't anybody flush in this house? The toilet was nearly filled and covered with flies. I gagged and spit into the sink, which was plastered with soap scum and wiped my mouth with a wadded up nasty towel. I stepped on an empty toilet paper roll and nearly lost my footing as I raced to the kitchen for some fresh air. One thing for certain, I never entered that house again. I didn't know which was worse, his mother or the living conditions. I think it was his mother. A house can always be cleaned.

Later back at the playground, Blackie wiggling around trying to get comfortable on a different tree root, one that was farther down from the elm tree. "Hey, Krame, do ya want another smoke?"

An older boy of twelve or so leaned up against the tree. "Where did youse guys get all those smokes?"

"Oh, fuck! You won't believe the system," Blackie said as I interrupted.

I nudged him. "Oh we just got lucky in the gutters yesterday. There isn't a system." But the kid didn't hear, or he wasn't listening. He was too busy combing his greased-down hair with his rat-tail comb and perfecting what pitiful little D.A. there was in the back.

I waited until the kid left to spill my guts. "Damn it, Blackie! *Don't* be telling anybody about this. Somebody will squeal and our ass is grass."

"Yeah, you're right as usual," he said as he fired several smoke rings onto a few roots. "I am so fucking bored. There's never anything to do. I can't wait till I'm older and get the hell out of here."

I nodded in agreement.

"I'll betcha I get out of here long before you do, Krame," he bragged.

"Yeah, Yeah. Hey, are we going to Municipal?" I asked. "Because if we are, we'd better get busy."

Blackie grinned. "You want inside or out?"

It only took a minute to decide. "I'll take inside. And don't get caught."

"Screw you. You just keep him busy," Blackie snapped back.

A few minutes later we were in position. I was in the front of Huey's store gazing at the new multi-colored jawbreakers, acting like I couldn't make up my mind which one to buy. Huey was behind the counter putting away packages of pencils, and there was a box of wide-spaced notebooks I knew he'd stock next.

"Let me know if I can help ya," he said politely.

"Oh, sure. I just don't know. They all look so good."

Meanwhile, Blackie had already lifted the hooked latch to the gate by the back alley. His long, skinny fingers had no difficulty reaching in between the vertical slats to unlock the only barrier between him and pay dirt. In a flash, he was inside the back storage area where Huey kept all the used pop bottles. I pictured Blackie down on his fingertips and toes, darting to the cases like a long-legged spider. In an instant, he had two cardboard six-packs of bottles in one hand and opening the gate to freedom with the other. He stole twelve bottles, which would equate to twenty-four cents, enough for the two of us to get into the pool.

"Hi, Huey," Blackie said as he entered the store with two empty bottles in each hand.

"How you doing, Blackie? I see you've been down by the drainage ditch at Audubon again. You are the luckiest kid for finding pop bottles." He took another look at him. "And you're filthy! I'll bet your mother will be really upset. Here, let me give you your eight cents."

"Thanks, Huey," he said as he scampered out the door.

"Well, did you make up your mind on the jawbreakers?" Huey asked.

"No, I'm going to have to think about it. See ya later," I told him.

A couple minutes later we were sitting on the fire escape, giggling at our stash of bottles and smoking a Pall Mall. We knew we could hit some other stores in the area to cash in the rest and have money left over after swimming.

I smoked like a pro, blowing smoke rings like an expert, enjoying this stolen freedom. "Ya know, I've been thinkin' about something else lately. I heard Crutchfield is still looking to beat me up for shooting the bird at him. He must be at least fourteen. Anyway, what I need is protection. I think we should form a gang and help each other out. A bunch of us together could take him."

"That's a great fuckin' idea!" Blackie yelled out. "Now that is what I'm talking about, Krame. *Krame* the *Brain*."

We all had nicknames based on our real names; Krame was short for my last name, Kramer. It was sort of a respect thing we did, I guess. Maybe it was because we had nothing better to do at that moment in our lives. Blackie was just Blackie and I couldn't imagine life without him.

Little did either of us know that within ten years, Blackie would be dead from a self-inflicted gunshot wound to the head.

Chapter Four: Eyelids

There he came. "Hey Rink!" I yelled to Kevin whose real last name was Rinniker.

"Hi, how are youse guys doing," he called out in typical Dubuque slang. "I been over to Eldora Reformatory and am sure glad to be back. Youse guys wouldn't believe how all those guys are watched all the time."

"Oh, screw 'em all," Blackie exclaimed. "If they're dumb enough to get caught, then fuck 'em."

Rink balled up his fist. "Hey, Blackie, one of them is my brother. That ain't so nice of you to say stuff like that."

Blackie looked pissed but stayed quiet.

"So why are ya glad to be back?" I asked.

Rink sighed. "At least here I can breathe! We were packed in the station wagon like sardines. There was eight of us kids. One good thing is I might have something to say in class when Sister Mary Alice asks us to speak up. God, I sure hate having to talk in class. I just ain't smart like *you*, Krame!"

"What the fuck does that mean?" Blackie jumped in.

Rink laughed. "Aw, nothing, just settle down or I'll have to crush you like I did last summer when you thought you could beat me up."

Rink was one year older than us and had been held back a grade in school. He was muscular for a kid of nine and was the joke of his third grade class because he was so much bigger and taller than the rest of us. His family was a typical Catholic one, having so many brothers and sisters, many of whom I knew only by sight. I couldn't even remember their names. They all looked alike.

A metal overhang hung off their house with a picnic table under it that his dad built for some of them to sit outside and eat when the weather allowed. I have no idea where all those kids ate when they were inside; like other kids I knew, I never went into his house. The house was way down the street, out of our neighborhood proper, backed up to Sacred Heart church. We'd play over there sometimes, riding sleds or passing by on the way to Comisky Park to ice skate in the winter.

"Hey, youse guys should see what I can lift now," Rink announced.

There were three activities in Rink's life that he enjoyed. One was helping the old women in the area. The second was hanging out with us. The third was weight lifting. He told us his old man was always telling the boys in the family to get strong in case of another big war like the one he'd fought in. He wanted his boys to be ready. From a block away, one could hear the clanking of metal as ten-pound weights were changed to fifty pounds when the older boys replaced the younger ones doing military presses or arm curls.

Mr. Rinniker had a cigar box full of medals from Okinawa and Saipan. None of us knew where those places actually were, but we did know, from him saying so, that he'd killed a lot of Japs there. Because he hated Japs, and because we didn't know any better, we did too. He would never tell us what happened over there despite our repeated questioning.

"So how much can ya pick up now?" Blackie prodded.

Rink flexed his muscles and puffed out his chest. "I can do twenty-five pounds thirty times without stopping."

"I guess ya think you're pretty fucking strong, huh?" Blackie asked.

"Yeah, I guess so."

Blackie gathered a big hawker of phlegm from deep in his chest, leaned back, and fired a slimy glob into the dirt at their feet. "Well then, pick that up," he commanded, as both Blackie and I laughed.

"Keep it up, wiseass," Rink said as he shook his head. "You'll see what happens."

He raised both hands to his right eyelid, and Blackie and I, knowing what was coming, immediately begged for mercy. "Aw Jesus, don't do that shit!" I pleaded.

Blackie looked the other way, his face pale. "Rink, you fucker, stop it. That gives me nightmares."

Rink turned his head toward us so we could get a real close look. 'Aw, shit!' I exclaimed as I saw how he'd flipped up his eyelid so it stayed stuck, inside out, with the red underside exposed for all to see. It was enough to make a guy want to throw up. This was a special trick only he could do. Once Father Michael beat him with a paddle for doing just that in class when several girls screamed, and the boys ran around the room trying to obtain a safe distance.

"Jesus, I hate that shit!" I said, as he rolled the lid back in place.

We all lit another Pall Mall and went to the elm tree. A moment later, there was Merle, and we began to serenade. In unison, and without any direction, we all hollered, "Poor Ole Merle, for the Worst is Yet to Come—Hey!"

He just gave us a dirty look, and we all laughed like we'd jut seen something hysterical on the Sunday night Ed Sullivan show. We fell suddenly silent, who knows what we were thinking, as we leaned into the tree, cradled by the majestic roots. Blackie blew smoke rings, Rink scratched at the dirt with a stick, and I hoped I wouldn't get beat up again when I got home that night.

Rink dusted himself off, dust flying in all directions. "Well, I'm going to see if Mrs. Lubbs needs help around the house. The other day when I delivered her groceries, she said something about needing the porch swept."

"Are you trying for some new fucking Cub Scout badge?" Blackie teased. "Why the shit are you always doing stuff for the old timers in the neighborhood?"

"My dad tells us to. He says something about sowing and reaping and a silver rule or something like that."

Blackie and I fell off our root perches, rolling in the dirt, and our laughter echoed off the schoolhouse as Rink walked away singing, "Poor Old Merle . . ."

"Can you believe that stupid ass doesn't know the Golden Rule," Blackie snipped. "My rule is 'Do unto others before they do it to you!'"

"But," I reminded him. "Only after you think it through. Look at all the things that could go wrong."

Blackie quickly jumped to another subject. "So when are we going to start that gang? And where the fuck is Bear?"

I ignored the question as I tore my shirt loose from the crusted-over blood on my back. I got whipped again last night and I swear they're getting harder all the time. It was strange to me how years later you can still pick at a scar, and feel the pain of the old wound, as if it were fresh. Sometimes I liked being quiet. This was one of those times.

Chapter Five: Safety

"Children, I'd like you to meet the newest member of our third grade class, Tommy Berry," Miss Phifner said. "Please welcome him."

"Hello, Tommy," we said in unison. He didn't reply but took a seat in the back row.

Anna Schwartz punched me in the back, but even at eight, I didn't need reminding. I craned my neck to look at the new kid with black-framed eyeglasses and long, greasy hair. I flipped my head in acknowledgement and he gave a short nod in return. I thought to myself that he might fit in with all us guys. He'd need a nickname though.

Later that day at recess, one of the kids yelled out, "Okay Krame, you and Unmacht are the captains, and Krame won the chicken claws, so he gets to pick first."

"Chicken claws" is where one person throws a baseball bat to another person and that person has to catch it. Then the one who threw the bat grabs his hand around it, above the one who caught it. One hand after another grasps the bat, until they got to the end of the bat. When one hand grasps directly under the knob, the other person gets to hold that knob with his fingers. The opponent then gets to kick it and if he knocks the bat out of his opponent's hand, then his team wins and gets first pick of team members. If the kid holding the bat doesn't drop it, then his team wins.

A boy named Markward spit in the grass. "Dammit, Krame. You always win!"

"Mr. Markward, watch your language," said Miss Coffee, the fifth grade teacher. She was the playground monitor that day.

We alternated picking who we thought would be the best players. "I pick Clemens first," I said as the rotation began.

There were just two kids left at the end. One was a fat kid named Sheffield and the other was the new kid named Tommy, who in my mind was already named Bear. He'd been watching from a distance over by the sidewalk and some fifty feet from home plate. I turned and yelled, "Hey you, Tommy, you're on my team. Come on over here."

I noticed he wasn't excited in the least, and didn't even run. He just pushed his glasses up onto the bridge of his nose and walked over with his head bent staring at the blacktop playground where our ball field was located.

"Okay, you have Sheffield," I said to the other captain as we gathered near home plate to decide who was going to play each position. I felt a touch on my right shoulder and looked to see Bear looking at me intently. "Hey, can I talk with you a minute?"

I nodded and we walked a few steps away. Bear swallowed hard. "I've never played baseball before. Just a little catch with my dad out in the front yard in Sherrill."

"What's Sherrill?" I asked.

"That's the town where we lived before moving here. I don't know what to do and I'd just as soon watch."

"No way, Bear, I want you on my team. I will help you and make sure you get by," I said.

"Who's Bear?" he asked.

"I'll tell you later. Now see that big elm tree out there by that fence with all the roots sticking up? That's called right field. After we bat and take the field, that's where I want you to go. It's just like playing catch. You catch the ball and throw it to the nearest kid yelling for the ball. You got it?"

"Okay, but I'm still scared," he said, swallowing hard.

It was the third inning when Bear had his first chance to bat. On the very first pitch, he hit that ball all the way out by the basketball pole that had been planted into the blacktop years before. He hit the backboard on the fly and took off running. Boys came from center and left fields to grab the ball and Bear was off, moving his legs so fast, he was a blur. His greasy black hair was whipping back and forth as he rounded the bases. *Holy crap*, I thought as he ran like the wind.

He got a standing double and immediately won the respect of the kids in the third grade. He was now one of us, and everybody started talking to him. He stood there on second base, looked over at me, and gave a wave as if say thanks for making him welcome.

After school, I pushed the long brass handle of the school door forward and shoved it open. "Hey, Krame," I heard someone say as I stepped outside onto the concrete stairs. I looked back to see Bear.

"Do you want to go to Huey's and share a pop?" he asked.

"Naw, but thanks. I don't have any money," I told him.

"I'll buy. It's my treat."

Moments later we were perched outside of Huey's, watching cars race up East 22nd Street and drunks stagger in and out of the Ten Spot Tavern across the street. We passed the bottle of pop back and forth.

"Hey, how'd you like that when I asked Miss Phifner to open the window 'cause I was hot?" I asked him and then took a swig of Pepsi.

"Yea, what was that all about?"

"Holy cow, didn't ya see it when she stood on the chair with the stick to open the upper window? I looked up her dress and saw where her nylons ended on her legs. Almost gave me a boner!"

He cackled. "Oh yeah, and I had to pick a seat way in the back! I'll ask her if I can move tomorrow."

Cackled, that was the operative word where Bear's voice was concerned. He had a giggle and laugh that sounded the same, sort of like a duck quacking. "Hey, what's with Bear? Why did you call me that?"

"We all have nicknames. My last name is Kramer, but everyone calls me Krame. Rink's last name is Rinniker, and your last name is Berry. So I thought we should call you Bear. Now, we also have Blackie," I explained.

"What's *his* last name?" Bear asked.

"It really is Weinerholter, but I wasn't about to call him Weiner."

Bear laughed and choked on his pop. I had to hit him on the back several times and then he continued laughing. "So why didn't you call him Dick for short?" We both cracked up.

I patted him on the shoulder. "I like how you think, Bear."

"Well, that's pretty neat! I never had a nickname before. Thanks," he said. "You sure did make me feel good today, picking me to be on your team. Thanks for that, too."

"That's okay," I said, feeling embarrassed somehow. "You looked pretty shy or scared or something just standing over there. And where did you get your speed? You're about the fastest runner I ever saw."

He took another sip. "I don't know. I was the fastest kid out in Sherrill, though."

"Where's Sherrill? I never heard of it."

"It's out on Highway 52 North, by Owl's Furniture Store where you turn back up in the country."

"I think that's the way we go to Decorah to visit my grandfather, my mom's dad," I said.

"Well it's nothing like Dubuque. It's a little town with one grocery store, two taverns, a welding shop and a volunteer fire department. My dad was a volunteer fireman out there."

I looked off to where he was pointing, as if I looked harder, I could see it all spread out before me. "Did you live in the country or in the city?"

"We lived in town but there were only about 300 people who lived there." He batted at a bee that had perched on his hand. "I went to a one-room school before coming to Audubon."

"What do you mean a one-room school?"

"Well, it had eight grades, and each grade had its own row. My two sisters also went there. They sat over a few rows because they're older. All of us were in the same room. We had an outhouse to use for a bathroom, and our recess was on a grassy area about the size of our infield today," he elaborated further.

I pinched my nose shut. "An outhouse! Ya mean where it's a little shack where there's no water and people just do their business into a hole?"

"Yeah," he said. "We had the same thing at home. And we had no running water until we moved to Kniest Street. This is the first time I used a toilet you flush. Or even turn on the faucet and get water to come out."

He looked down at the ground. "Please don't tell the other kids about that 'cause I don't want them to think I'm some kind of hick or something. Okay?"

"I won't say a word, Bear," I promised.

He grinned. "Bear. I like that name."

"Hey watch this," I said as the Linwood bus made its regular stop in front of Huey's.

Neither of us were bothered by the cloud of exhaust as the bus pulled away leaving a middle-aged woman standing at the corner. Her name was Georgia, and she was a bit slow. She was a kind and polite person who lived with her sister above Weise's Meat Store, next to Sacred Heart church. She always wore a brightly colored dress that stopped between her knees and ankles. She walked with a slight shuffle, and wore heavy looking black shoes. She carried her purse across her chest, hooked across both arms like it held some secret treasure. She clomped across the brick street, and as she stepped up onto the sidewalk I yelled, "Hiya, Georgia."

She turned around and faced us, releasing the grip on her purse with her right arm and waving rapidly. "Hiya, boys."

"Hey, Georgia, your slip is showing!" I taunted.

She bent her elbow and flicked her wrist and yelled back, "Oh, shut up."

Bear about choked on his pop as it fired out his nostril, he laughed so hard. Every kid in the neighborhood at one time or another had picked on Georgia. The funny part was, we would have defended her or helped her in any way, at any time.

"Oh my god, that was too funny. I have to try that some time," Bear said, handing the bottle back to me for another swig.

"So it's the truth, you had a real outhouse?" I asked.

"Yeah, no shit. We actually had two. One for Dad and me and the other for my sisters and my Ma. We had a cistern that hooked to a pump in the kitchen and we had to boil water on the coal stove to drink it. Once a week we'd all take a bath in a big metal tub after Ma would boil the water and Dad would carry it outside for us to bathe. Ma always waited until after dark to take her bath. Rain or snow, we all walked to school about a mile every day. I feel like I'm living in Chicago being here in Dubuque," he finished.

I shook my head in amazement. "Holy cow, that is some story."

"Now you promise not to tell the other kids at school, will ya?" he asked again.

"Scout's honor," I said as I gave the Cub Scout salute.

"What's that?" he asked.

"Have you never heard of Scouts? We get together and make stuff and have lots of fun. Ask your ma and dad if you can join. I'll take you with me next week if you want."

"Boy, this has been such a good day," he said as he took the last swig of pop and put it down on the sidewalk between his legs.

I thought of something else to tell him. "Oh yeah, there's one more thing you should know. Ya remember that big elm tree out in right field where you played today? That's where we hang out and smoke, cuss, and best of all, sing to Merle, the janitor at school. It's far enough away that we can run down the street if Merle comes after us, but its safe from all the neighborhood drunks."

"Yeah," Bear said looking interested.

"Now, something you should know, don't ever sit up close to the base of the tree when the older guys are around. Ya know, like the ten-and twelve-year-old kids," I said as he listened intently.

Once again he pushed his glasses up his nose, ran his fingers through his hair, leaned forward on the cement stoop. "Why not?"

"The base of the tree is taken by the older kids. They'll beat you up if you're in their spot. If you do have it, and one comes walking up, just move down on the roots where you belong. It's a sign of respect. They will like ya then," I told him.

He shrugged. "So what's with the singing? Why do you sing to the janitor and what do you sing?"

"We sing 'Poor Ole Merle, for the Worst is Yet to Come—Hey!'" I said as I sang the tune for him.

He let out his usual cackle, and asked why we did that.

"Because we've always done that, that's why," I said. "Kids who now drive cars and are long gone from here have done it, and probably kids before that. It's just a tradition. For me it's a way of picking on an adult who can't get even, and it sure feels good."

Bear slapped me on the shoulder. "Jeez, this day is getting better every minute. I got to play baseball, share a pop with you, Krame, watch you tease Georgia, and now learn a new song."

I cocked my head and looked him in the eyes. "Now, I told you I'd never tell anyone about how you lived in Sherrill, right?"

He nodded in agreement. "I have something special to tell you that you can never tell anyone unless I say its okay. Do you agree?"

Bear returned the frank-eyed look. "Sure, what is it?"

I didn't start my story with "Once upon a Time" but I might as well have, the way Bear paid such close attention. "I live in a really old house that was built over a hundred years ago, and down in the cellar there's a special place."

"Holy crap," he said, his mouth hanging open. "What . . . is it?"

I lowered my voice like I was with the CIA. "We have a big trunk used a long time ago for storing stuff. The bottom comes out of it and there is a trap door. If I open the trap door and lift it up, there's a ladder that goes down below the street and into a secret city."

Bear's eyebrows rose over the rim of his glasses. "Oh, wow! Can I see it sometime?"

"Maybe later," I said. "Anyway, there's an ice cream shop, a Ferris wheel, a music shop with people singing, a place where you can ride horses, and a free shooting gallery like at the county fair. Maybe sometime I will take you down there. I go there a lot in my mind when my dad beats me in the basement."

"What do you mean he beats you in the basement," he said, looking so serious, I wished I hadn't mentioned the beatings.

I let out a little laugh. "Oh nothing. I just made that part up."

"Hey, do you want to go to my house and meet my folks? We can get another pop or some Kool-Aid."

"Great. Okay," I said as we walked back into Huey's to return the pop bottle, and then we were off to Bear's house.

"How was school today, Tommy?" Mrs. Berry asked.

"Good, Ma. This is my new friend, Krame," he said as he opened the refrigerator. "Krame, do ya want a Pepsi?" he asked as he already pulled two from the cardboard six-pack carton. "He gave me a new nickname. It's Bear, short for Berry. Get it?"

"Sure, I'll have one if it's okay with your mother."

"Oh, Krame, any friend of Tommy's is a friend of the family. Mac will love that one," she said as she set another shirt on the counter, among a row of other shirts neatly rolled and sprinkled with water, ready to be ironed.

Bear cackled. "Yeah, my dad even sounds like a bear, so I guess we'll keep it all in the family."

Mrs. Berry was so short she could hardly reach the ironing board even though she had it raised only half way. She was doing some of the day's chores. She shook a brown bottle of water that once was home to Dubuque Star beer and now had a stopper in it that allowed the water to sprinkle onto the dry clothes before she pressed the hot iron to them. On the back of the door to the basement was a large hook, now holding several pair of pressed blue jeans. Stacks of white T-shirts, also pressed and folded, were sitting on the counter. The kitchen cupboards were white metal and the counter top was red with white doors beneath. There was a big refrigerator and a new stove lined up against the walls. I felt so relaxed and comfortable swigging my Pepsi, I felt like I'm come home. Then it all came to a halt.

"Who the hell are you?" Mr. Berry asked when he came in from the back porch after another day at John Deere. He glared at us and set his black lunch pail on the kitchen table.

The deep, powerful, gravelly voice almost made me shit my pants just like Jim Clay's dad when we were throwing balls against Huey's Store wall. Before I could speak, Mrs. Berry saved me.

"Oh, Mac, this is a friend of Tommy's from school. His name is Kramer—but everybody calls him Krame. He lives up the street on Lincoln and has six brothers and sisters. He even gave Tommy a new nickname today. It's Bear," she told him.

He took off his cap. "Well, you're not staying for supper, are ya?"

"No, Mr. Berry. I can't stay for supper," I said as he put out his hand and shook mine.

"Just call me Mac," he said as he turned to open the refrigerator to retrieve a Hamm's beer. He glanced at Bear. "How was school, son?"

"Aw, just great, dad. I was picked by Krame to be on his baseball team, I learned a new song, and do ya know what's in the basement at Krame's house?" he said as I kicked him under the table. "Tomorrow I'm asking our teacher if I can move my seat over next to the windows," he said excitedly and gave me a wink.

Mac wasn't listening as he was enjoying his beer and gave out a huge, rattling belch. Both of us kids just laughed.

"Well, I'm glad you had fun and have a new friend," Mac continued, "So you fellas have nicknames, huh? You are such a little shit," he said, pointing at me. "I'll give you another nickname. From now on, we'll call you Twink," he said, and laughed to himself.

Tommy had told me about his dad at recess earlier that day. He had served in WW II as an MP, and at one time, guarded President Truman and General Eisenhower when they had some kind of meeting. He even showed me a photograph on the playground that day.

But that first day, in their kitchen, the first thing I noticed about both was how each would push their eyeglass frames up their noses with their left hands. Mac's frames were black like Tommy's. Now,

Tommy also had this habit of flipping his head in a jerk to the right to keep his hair in place. Mac didn't need to bother, as he was bald, except for the sides.

"So are ya ready to go to work, Ma?" he asked Mrs. Berry, who by now was putting away the ironing board.

"I guess," she said with a little giggle.

All of a sudden he raised his right leg up and let out with a thunderous fart that almost rattled the glasses in the cupboard. It must have lasted five seconds or more. I choked on my Pepsi and it came shooting out my nose. There was a stinging in my nose from either carbonation or methane gas. I wasn't sure which. But one thing I knew for sure; Blackie's dad was my kind of guy.

"Jeez Dad, that was a good one!" Bear cackled.

Mrs. Berry laughed and shook her head. "Oh Mac, quit teaching those kids bad habits."

She worked the night shift at the Dubuque Pack and Mac always drove her to work at 4:30 sharp. Then, when he returned, Bear, his sisters, and Mac all sat down to a hot meal, either from the oven or off the stove that Mrs. Berry had prepared earlier. This was a ritual that lasted for years.

"I suppose you *are* eating with us?" Mac asked when he returned from taking Mrs. Berry to work. "I was just kidding earlier."

"No, if I'm not home by five o'clock I'll really get it from my dad."

"Anytime, Twink. You're always welcome here. I want you to know that son. Anytime."

As I took the porch steps two at a time in my rush to get home, I remembered thinking how I not only had a new best friend; I had a new best *family*. That was in the spring of 1957.

Boy, this is a great day, I thought as I sprinted up Lincoln Avenue to get home before five o'clock supper. Then I saw it and my stomach dropped. Dad was already home and his car was parked outside. I felt sick in an instant, knowing what was in store for me. I stopped and vomited in Mrs. Cierney's front lawn. I was in deep trouble.

"Where the Christ have you been?" Bushy asked.

"I thought . . . " I tried to say but was interrupted.

He popped me a good one. "You thought, my ass. You never think. You know what to do. Get the hell out of here," he said as my brother asked for someone to begin passing the chicken potpies.

They were just starting supper. I must have just missed the deadline. I entered the stairway to the cellar and flipped on the light. I stepped past the mop, dustpan and broom to go down the stairs to the room where the washer and dryer were sitting, side-by-side like mute witnesses. I pulled down the chain hooked to the bare light fixture in the far room and sat on the cold cement floor waiting for supper to be done upstairs. I glanced over to where the imaginary trunk was sitting above the city below, and wished I were somewhere else having an ice cream cone.

The scraping of the metal chair against the linoleum on the kitchen floor above brought me back to reality as I heard Bushy descending the stairs. He'd already removed his belt.

"Alright, move it. You know the position. You also know we eat supper every night at five o'clock. You know what happens now."

I began crying before he even started, hoping this time tears would save me. But they did not. I grabbed my ankles and didn't flinch an inch at the burning sting from the belt's hot leather. One, two, three, four, five, six . . . ten strikes I counted. That was the rule for being late.

Chapter Six: Black Walls

A few days later, Sacred Heart's bells were clanging six-o'clock and I charged down the alley, shooting at make-believe Japs and Krauts hiding behind and next to the wooden single-car garages. A couple times I was hit by gunfire, fell and rolled on the only available patch of grass, in the yard of Mrs. Cierney. I remember seeing grass clippings on my shirt from where Rink had cut the grass earlier in the day. I didn't care, 'cause I was winning the war.

A few houses away I turned the corner and raced across Johnson Street toward the elm tree. I saw Bear getting punched in the arm by Blackie and Rink and knew he'd just lost another episode of rock, paper, scissors. When we were bored (which was most of the time) one game we played was rock, paper, scissors. Whoever lost was on the receiving end of a punch from the others.

"Ow. Not so hard, Blackie," I heard Bear say as he rubbed his left arm and fell off the root into the dirt. "That *hurt!*"

I sprayed him with dust as I did a sideways slide, turned, and fired a parting shot at the last Jap hiding across the street in the alley. "So, what'd you have, Bear?" I asked, as he was perched again on the small root, a space that was just the right size for his butt.

"Aw nuts, I had rock, but those two had paper." He rubbed his arm. "So both of 'em got their punch in on me. Only Blackie hit me really hard."

The perpetrator held his teeth together and shot a spray of spit out between them onto the dust. "Ya better quit whining, or I'll give ya something to whine about." All four of us laughed at the mockery Blackie made in reference to our fathers' almost daily threats.

"So youse must have had cleanup tonight, huh?" Rink asked.

What he was referring to was the order of washing the nightly dishes after supper at our house. Ma couldn't do them at all as she said the soap made her arthritis hurt, and standing there so long made her legs cramp. So, from the time each of us was about three years old, we started a routine that would last until we left home to be on our own.

The first of my siblings to yell out their choice of dish duty won and the others would yell what they wanted next. Clean up was first. It was a messy job, but whoever chose it, was finished first. Washing took longer and there was always the threat that Bushy'd come out to inspect and scream at you if he found any leftover food on the dishes or silverware. The good part about washing was you could place the dishes just so into the rubber-coated strainer so as not to fall, but in such a way as whoever dried them had to think about which dish to remove first. It was kind of like a house of cards, or a game of pick-up sticks.

The washer always tried to make a dish fall as the drier did their job. Boy, those Melmac plates really rattled when dropped, even on linoleum. It was a game we all played, even into our later teens before moving out. The drier wiped each dish, utensil, pot, and pan with a thin cloth that had long ago lost its color. When the last item was put away, it was always soaked as there was not a dry spot to be found on the towel. Drying and also putting them away was the most difficult. It took longer, and god forbid if we ever dropped anything, or even worse, broke something. Once I broke an empty Kraft's Grape Jelly jar that was now being used as a drinking glass. The next night I had to do all the dishes by myself. In addition to the house of cards game, there was one more game I personally played against my brother Mark.

Whenever he lost and had to dry, he developed a sudden urge to be in our only working bathroom. He would sit on the throne for an hour, reading the *Des Moines Register* while the dishes were drying themselves. I would hang around and wait for the sound of the toilet flushing. Then, like a surgeon cutting on a body, I would weave in and out of every dish and spray them with fresh water. I even filled the jelly jars all the way to the top. When I heard him unlatch the bathroom hook that locked the door, I would run out the back. And so it was a chore we each accepted and never questioned that it had to be done, and done right.

"Krame! Are youse deaf or what?" Rink asked while Blackie offered me a drag on his smoke.

"Oh, no. Sorry," I replied. "Just thinking. Mark had to do all the dishes tonight as punishment for being three minutes late for supper. I sure am glad he can't run as fast as me, cause I always go into my Jesse Owens speed when I see the old man's car coming home at suppertime. Ya know how we have to eat exactly at five o'clock? Anyway, Mark was late because he had to get medicine for Ma up at Ruegnitz Drug Store and missed the starting time. So he got the usual. No supper, had to sit in the basement while we ate, then ten licks with the belt and had to do all the dishes. Good for me," I told the gang as I blew a smoke ring against the tree.

"Old man Kupperschmidt almost got me yesterday," Bear interrupted. "I had three of his best apples rolled up in my shirt and was eating a fourth when he came charging out with his rifle. He shot, and I heard the salt hit Chauncey's metal garage door. I dropped 'em, but kept the one I was eating and got away. I saw some old lady hanging laundry in your back yard, Krame, as I ran down here. Then I got the green apple two-step and had to go home and drop a load. I guess it wasn't ripe yet," he finished.

Kupperschmidt didn't need a long-handled picker or a bunch of migrants to retrieve his apples from the tree. Every kid in the neighborhood would see to it that his crop disappeared. Whenever he saw us out there stealing his fruit, he'd charge out of the screen door with his rock salt-filled weapon and he would fire away. There were indeed times when some slow poke would get nailed in the butt and welt up pretty good. The rest of us would just laugh at him. Mark was hit once in the upper thigh and butt area because he lost his footing on the rocks in the alley. All of us knew better than to tell our dads, as we'd get in trouble for stealing. That was the only time Mark actually had to dry dishes as they were being washed. He never read the *Des Moines Register* after supper that night. It hurt too much to sit.

"So who was that white haired lady hanging clothes in your yard yesterday?" Bear asked.

"Oh, that's Grandma Kramer from Cedar Falls. My Uncle Matt drove her here," I said. "Ma is sick again and Grandma's here helping out. Ma doesn't look sick, but all she does is stay in bed and smoke one cigarette after another. And if she's not smoking, she just lies there staring and ignores all of us. Dr. Melgard said a few weeks of rest and more medicine and she'll be fine."

"Yeah, I saw your grandmother a couple months ago when I was cutting Ms. Cierney's lawn. She was doing the laundry then too," Rink said.

"Oh, that reminds me. You guys aren't gonna believe this one!" I exclaimed. "Yesterday, when we finished playing baseball, and everybody went home for lunch, I saw the most gawd-awful thing! Grandma had set a cup of bleach on the back of the bathroom sink because she likes to mix bleach with water and let the dirty white clothes soak in the sink for a while. Anyway, she had this cup of bleach sitting near the sink, and Mark raced in and was so thirsty he didn't even notice—he grabbed the cup of bleach, thinking it was water and gulped it down just as I was walking by. I saw and heard the most explosive black vomit come shooting out of him, all over the wall, the floor, the sink, and part of the toilet. It slid down the wall to the baseboard and just clung there. Where he fired it at the toilet, it was so thick, it took several seconds to reach the floor after clinging to the side of the bowl. He turned in panic and more vomit shot out at the sink and covered the cold-water knob and slid into the sink. The smell was worse than any dead animal." They knew I exaggerated from time to time, but even I had to admit, I'd outdone myself on this one.

Everybody talked at once. Their eyes were as big as those purple Melmac plates. Bear had his hand over his mouth, Blackie choked on smoke, and Rink's mouth was wide open.

"Why was it black?" Rink asked.

"Damn, did he go to the hospital? Did he lose some of his guts?" Blackie said at the same time.

Bear could barely get a word in edge-wise. "What did your old lady do . . . what'd *you* do?"

"I know you guys have never been in my house, but Ma and Dad's bedroom is right next to the bathroom. It's between the kitchen and the living room. I yelled for Ma, but she just lay on her side, smoking. She never reacted at all. So I ran out in the back yard and yelled for Grandma, who came running to help. As Grandma grabbed the phone to call the doctor, the cord hit all of Ma's medicine bottles and they scattered everywhere. There must have been fifteen of them. Dr. Melgard's office told Grandma to have Mark drink something, and then after that drink lots of water. The smell was like nothing I ever smelled before. But the way the vomit shot all the way across the bathroom was pretty scary. The black color was just nasty. I almost got sick."

"So, is he okay now?" Bear asked.

"Damn, what do you think, you stupid ass," Blackie snorted "God, I wouldn't move for days if that happened to me."

"Yeah," I said disgustedly. "After Grandma took care of him, he went upstairs and slept all afternoon. When he got up he said it was no big deal. It was a good thing Grandma was there to help because Ma just rolled over in the bed. I guess she was too tired to notice."

Chapter Seven: Bombs Away

A few days later we were back at the elm tree. Blackie spit a big hocker at the elm and it clung for a moment, then slid down the bark. "Where the fuck is Bear?"

"He went to the car wash with Mac," I said. "He should be around in a while."

"Jesus, am I sore," said Rink, as he came up to the tree, fixing his tight shorts and wiggling his shoulders as if to get out of his tank top.

I slapped him on the back. "Were ya lifting again today? How are ya doing? Your whole family sure takes this shit seriously. Have ya seen any Japs yet?"

"Very funny," he said, rubbing his lower back. "No, I'm sore because I carried three bags of groceries from Entringer's Grocery Store, up four blocks to Mrs. Johnson's. They were really heavy with all that canned stuff. Then I helped the Udelhovens move some furniture into a pickup truck. Did youse guys know they were moving?"

None of us responded as Bear rounded the corner, licking a raspberry ice cream cone he'd just bought at Huey's with his allowance. He was the only kid in the neighborhood who received an allowance. With both parents working, it was no wonder. Every other mother stayed home in the late 50s.

Bear stuck out his hand. "Anybody want a lick?"

"Fuckin' right!" Blackie yelled, as he jumped up and took a bite.

Rink and I took turns taking a mouthful, and before we knew it, the cone was demolished. But Bear didn't care; he always shared whatever he had. We all leaned back against the empty tree wishing we had some ice water to quench our sudden thirst. The desire was satisfied when Blackie offered us each a Pall Mall.

Halfway through our smokes, Rink asked Blackie if "he'd found it." Bear and I exchanged puzzled glances. Unbeknownst to us, Blackie and Rink had concocted a scheme of a never-before attempted feat in all of Audubon's history. The two of them went off to the far corner of the school near the back entrance and returned with Blackie rolling a huge inner tube he'd previously stolen from the junkyard down the street. It was from a smashed truck that had slammed into the hillside along Highway 52 on its way to Decorah. The driver was killed and there was little left of the semi. After the wrecking company received the call, dads and kids alike gathered to see the mangled metal.

In the middle of the night, Blackie had gone next door to the junkyard and removed the inner tube from the pile of truck parts. Always thinking, he rolled it the two blocks up to Audubon and hid it behind the bushes, under the third-grade class window where Miss Phifner had exposed here nylons to my more than willing eyes

Now, under our watchful eyes, Blackie grew tired of rolling the tube on the dirt playground and gave it to Rink for his turn. Rink turned the corner and headed up the three-story fire escape with the inner tube.

Bear looked puzzled. "What the hell are they doing?"

"Who knows?" I said angrily, feeling miffed that I'd been left out of whatever was going on.

"Is this okay?" Blackie hollered up to Rink, fifty feet above. "Can ya get me from here?"

"Youse need to move over to your left," Rink said, as he balanced the mass of rubber on its side. "Okay, that's good—here we go!"

Just then I saw what these two morons were trying to do. Rink yelled, "Bombs away!" as he shoved the tube towards a waiting Blackie below.

I ran as fast as I could to save my friend, Blackie, from what would most certainly be imminent death from the crushing blow of the rubber tube smashing his skull. Bear was not far behind as we both screamed for Blackie to move, to get the hell outta there.

Blackie just stood there, waiting to be encircled by the rubber glob. But instead of it staying on course and circling his body when it landed, the tire changed its position halfway down. Some ten feet away, I heard it as it hit straight onto his skull, collapsing his small frame to the hardened dirt beneath. As if doing an encore, the tire bounced again several times onto his lifeless body. These two assholes thought they could circle Blackie with the inner tube from high above and not get hurt. Good grief!

Taking three steps at a time down the fire escape, Rink was screaming, "Oh, shit! I'm so sorry. I'm coming, Blackie."

Blackie's body twitched and jerked, but otherwise, he didn't respond. It was as if he was fighting a nightmare in his sleep. I was the first one to his side and tried to wake him. He fluttered in the dirt for a moment and the chipped front tooth was all I saw as he gasped for breath. Bear shoved the inner tube off his chest and immediately all of us circled him.

After what seemed like hours, but was probably only a few minutes, Blackie opened his eyes and looked around. "What the fuck happened?"

All three of us were yelling and screaming at him for being such a stupid son of a bitch and saying that he could have been killed. He didn't yell back, just sat up, looking at his torn and tattered shoes, and said he had to go home. He said he felt really tired. And he did all of that without once using the F-word.

A few days later we saw Blackie again. He had multiple bruises all over his arms and the lower parts of his legs. I asked if that was from the inner tube.

"Naw. I told Ma what happened that day and first she beat me with the strap and then used a piece of wood on me. I told her how tired I was and she called Dr. Melgard. He said I probably had a concussion and not to let me sleep for at least an hour. So she beat me some more." He eyed me knowingly. "You get how *that* goes, don't ya Krame?"

"You stupid sons-a-bitches," I yelled. "How many times have I told ya to think of every possible thing that could go wrong before you do something? That way, nothing bad happens. You guys need to ask me before you try another dumb-ass trick like that!"

"Yea, f'ing right, Krame. You are the thinker," Blackie said, rubbing his chin. "Why is that?"

"Simple," I said. "It's called survival."

Some two weeks later, the incident of Firestone meets Blackie was forgotten. It was so stinking hot and humid that summer of 1957; each of us could barely lift a Pall Mall to our lips. Thanks to Blackie's new talent, we seldom had to check the gutters along the streets for used cigarette butts. We had collected enough revenue, compliments of Huey, to go swimming at Municipal Pool.

"Do youse guys want to hitch hike or walk all the way up there?" Blackie asked.

Bear said there must be a better way, and Rink agreed. It was just too hot for the one-mile hike.

"Naw," I said, feeling excited. "I've been thinking the last several nights about something we could do and it seems foolproof."

Blackie let out a long whistle. "Krame, you are always thinking and are always up to something. Fuck, don't ya ever sleep?"

"Naw, not much. Ya never know what will happen at night," I blurted out and realized what would be said next.

All three laughed and shoved each other, until Bear fell off a big root, all the while Blackie taunting: "Aw, the mean old boogie man will get ya, huh?"

"No, the old man," I said, staring at the dirt. All laughter stopped for a few minutes.

Rink put a hand on my shoulder. "So what's this plan you have for us?"

"Yeah," Bear said, narrowing his eyes. "And how do ya know we won't get caught?"

Blackie offered a thumbs-up. "Yeah, I'm glad we didn't tell him our plan with the truck inner tube or that fucker would have stopped us."

"I guess I learned it from the Old Man or because of the Old Man," I said, tucking my hands in my armpits. "If ya get caught or mess up, there'll be a beating waiting for ya. I've had enough to know we all need to plan and scheme so we don't get the shit kicked out of us."

"Not in my house," Bear said, but not in a bragging way.

"Yea, that is so true," I said, agreeing because I'd seen it firsthand. "You have the best parents in the neighborhood." The other two nodded in agreement.

"So what's your idea, Krame?" Rink asked.

"We know the trains like the back of our hands. We know the Milwaukee Road heads north every afternoon. Why not go over to Garfield Avenue and hop on? It's flat. We can all run fast," I said, sort of speed talking.

The other looked interested so I continued. "We can hop a flat car when the railroad dicks aren't looking and then jump off somewhere up by the Point Restaurant."

"Unless Blackie's shoes rip apart," Rink said as he and Bear cackled.

"Screw you," Blackie mumbled. "I'll be just fine. See, that's what I'm talking about, Krame! You're always thinking. How long you been planning this little trick?"

"Yea, when did youse get this great idea? I'll do it," Rink said, his eyes over-bright. "I can easily pull myself up on the car."

Bear was more sullen. "I don't know guys, we could get hurt, or even killed."

"Oh fuck you," Blackie yelled, kicking at the dirt. "Maybe you could take a cab with your allowance."

I shoved Blackie hard. "Hey, kiss my ass, you son of a bitch! Leave him alone," I said feeling suddenly protective.

We stood around a while, looking at each other, tossing insults back and forth, like normal.

Finally, Rink got serious. "So, are we gonna do it? Let's go home and get changed into our trunks and meet by the trains over by Garfield. This'll be fun."

Chapter Eight: The Jellyfish Float

Bear tossed his head and straightened his glasses after pulling himself up onto the flatcar. "Boy, that wasn't hard at all. It was barely moving."

"See, I told you guys it would be easy, and there was no sign of railroad dicks at all," I remarked as I pulled the webbing of my trunks out of my butt crack.

We watched the top of Marshall Elementary School whizzing past us. "Hey, how fast do youse guys think we're going?" Rink yelled.

Blackie sat trying to fix his left shoe. He looked up nervously. "Fuck, we need to plan our jump-off point 'cause this thing is really speeding!"

I didn't say a word but just let the others worry for several minutes. I enjoyed all the looks of near terror on their faces. I felt in total control and it was a powerful feeling for a change. Weeks earlier I'd heard the old man telling Ma how the city made the railroad slow to a crawl up by Municipal, near Spahn & Rose Lumber Company, because there were too many kids running around the crossing gates to scamper over to the pool. I soon told my friends this and moments later they were all laughing and shoving one another about how brave we all were after hopping off of the flatcar. A bum stood in a passing boxcar and gave me a salute as he passed by. I returned the respect and was proud of another successful Krame caper.

"Hey, what do youse say we get out of here and go up to Flat Rock and swim?" Rink asked.

Boredom had set in at the pool as we performed jackknives and cannon balls for over an hour. We splashed all the girls and dunked kids smaller than us. Blackie returned to our group after sitting on the hot cement as he was put in a fifteen-minute penalty zone for telling a lifeguard to get screwed.

"I guess so," Bear responded, half-heartedly.

"You guess so, what? You fucker," he asked, grinning so wide, his slashed tooth was exposed for everyone to see.

"Rink was just saying how we might go up to flat rock and swim rather than sticking around here. What do you think?" I asked

Blackie who looked cleaner than I had seen him in weeks. It's amazing what chlorine water does to clean up a person.

"That's gross!" some older girls screamed as Rink turned around with his eyelids rolled up on top of each other.

"Awe, ya idiot, stop that. Jesus, I hate when you do that shit!" Blackie yelled.

"You'll regret it when they stay like that. My dad says when I make faces in the mirror, one day I'll be all twisted and stuff," Bear scolded.

"We know, we know," we said in unison, as though we'd practiced it.

"So, what do youse guys think? Are we gonna go or not?"

"Yea. Let's do it," I said.

Moments later an idea hit me like never before. There was no planning, no scheming, and for the first time I didn't consider getting the belt if we got caught. I suppose I was still basking in my success with the train hop. "Oh my god, I have a great idea! This will be so good!" I said as I brought everyone to a halt.

"What the fuck now?" Blackie asked.

Bear flipped his wet hair to the right and cackled, "Oh, I don't like the sounds of this already."

Rink stopped in his tracks. "What do you got in mind, Krame? Did youse think this through? How come we're just now hearing about it?"

Standing next to the railroad tracks, I had to yell over the passing cars and heavy machinery working over at the lumberyard. All the men were busy putting away a load of new lumber and there was one guy with a green hard hat barking orders at the others.

What a prick, I thought. *He doesn't have to be so mean to those guys.*

"So what's your idea?" Bear said, interrupting my thoughts.

I made a motion like a light bulb going on over my head. "Oh yea, how about we steal a plank of wood from the yard and haul it up to Flat Rock? We can use it for a diving board."

"Youse have to be nuts! We'll get caught for sure. They'll send us to Eldora. No, I don't want to do this," Rink stated.

"My dad's never laid a hand on me, but he would if they catch us. This could be bad," Bear said, sounding scared.

"Holy fuck! This is the best one yet, Krame. Let's do it. Oh shit, we will be the talk of the tree," Blackie said, jumping up and down.

"Blackie, you can't say a word. Those older guys at Audubon will tell our dads and then all of us will catch it. Do you understand?" I demanded.

Blackie nodded and crossed his heart. "Yea, this will be so much fun. Think of the good time we'll have diving off into the river."

"So when did you think this up? How long has this been in the works?" Bear asked.

"Just now," I said, as everything came to a hush.

"What the fuck," Blackie said, standing his ground. "You never gave this any thought? You *always* think shit through."

"Aw, this just can't be good, Krame," Bear said as Rink nodded in agreement.

"Okay, here's my plan. Those guys are so busy over there they won't notice the four of us taking a short cut through the building. Look at 'em. There're all being yelled at by the prick in the green helmet. This will work; I can feel it. We have to walk in like we own the place. Just go up there where all that wood is. Rink, you are tall enough and strong enough to pull out a plank. The three of us will stand guard and yell if anyone's coming, and then we just run up the tracks at the far end."

"What will youse yell?" Rink said.

"How about 'run you dumb fucker'?" Blackie said while Bear cackled like a young hyena.

"Rink," I instructed. "You take the front of the plank, and the rest of us will fall in behind. That way, you can see best, because of your height. Do not run. Remember, they have to think we bought it. Remember, we own the place. Just keep telling yourselves that, and this will work."

Not one word was spoken as we marched toward the huge open door until I heard Bear behind me saying, "Oh jeez. Aw, *jeez*."

"Shut the fuck up, Bear," Blackie said, clapping him on the shoulder. "We own the place!"

Moments later, with hearts pounding and each of us sweating as if it had been years since we'd been in the cool water at Municipal Pool, the weight of the plank now extended over our heads. While we didn't run, we certainly did walk at a quickened pace toward the far gate and up onto Rhomberg Avenue. The closer we got to the street, the more our muscles relaxed.

"Oh my god!" Bear said. "That scared the shit out of me. That was so exciting, and nobody even noticed us!"

"Krame, you are a fucking wizard," Blackie yelled. "You were right. They didn't even see us. It was like we weren't even there. Holy shit, my heart's still pounding!"

"Hey, do youse guys want to carry this on our sides now?" Rink asked.

At that moment I felt like a king. I remember hoping the guy in the green hard hat would get his ass chewed out when they discovered the missing piece of wood. *There is no reason to pick on people, except for Merle the janitor*, I thought and then began to sing.

"Poor Ole Merle, for the Worst is Yet to Come—Hey!" We sang at the top of our lungs as we left civilization behind, carrying our trophy to the banks of the Mississippi River.

"Raise it up higher, Rink. Ya almost have it. There, everybody shove it in," I directed as we plunged the diving board over one rock and under another.

"Looks like it's wedged in there real good. Let's test it," Bear said.

"Geronimo!" Rink yelled as he flew into the air and out into the brown water after several good bounces on the board.

We knew that if the board safely held him, it would surely hold each of us. One by one we took turns doing more cannonballs and leaps into the water. Flat Rock was a thick piece of limestone that jutted out from the steep bank, bordered above by the railroad tracks, and met the river's edge below. One hundred miles north of us lay Minnesota and directly across the river was Wisconsin. While we played in the murky, muddy waters, some fifty feet out from our swimming hole was the border of the locks where boats passed through.

"Hey youse guys, look at this," Rink yelled as we all cussed at him for doing that eyeball thing again. "I have a great idea if a train comes by while we're here!"

"You with a great idea? That'll be the day, you asshole," Blackie yelled, holding onto the plank while swooshing his legs back and forth in the water.

Rink continued telling his idea, and we each grinned in excitement. This would indeed be hilarious when and if a train came by. We took turns dunking each other, splashing, and picking on each other for a while. There were more cannonballs and an occasional boat blew its horn at us after passing through the locks. And then, we heard it, the roaring of an engine clickety-clacking along the tracks.

Bear immediately stopped his rough housing. "Holy cow! I hear a train coming!"

My heart felt like it leapt to my throat. "So do I. Everybody get in your places! Are you ready, Rink?"

That damn fool could barely swim out to the middle of the river's cut that separated us from the lock as he was too busy laughing. We were all laughing. Finally in place, he yelled back to us, "Okay—tell me when."

Growing up with trains passing a mere ten feet from some of our homes, we knew a railroad worker would be hanging out of the caboose window; it was always that way. Sometimes he'd wave to us, and sometimes he'd shoot us the bird if we peppered him with water balloons. This train would be no different.

Blackie crawled up the bank on his belly and hid in some scrub bushes that separated the tracks from the river below. We knew he could 't be heard with the train passing inches away, so he was to give me a sign and I would pass it on to Rink. The ground shook and rumbled, and rocks were fired past our heads as the speeding locomotive raced by. Trains usually had some 120 cars and took about eight minutes to clear a crossing, depending on its speed.

Blackie gave the sign and I cupped my hands over my mouth and yelled as loud as I could. "Okay, Rink —here it comes!"

"Oh shit. This is going to be so good," Bear cackled as the two of us hid under the plank, holding the sides for support.

Just then, Rink pulled off his swimming trunks, grabbed his ankles, held his breath and went under the water. There it was—a perfect jellyfish float! All we could see was his white ass bobbing in the brown, murky Mississippi River, nothing but two cheeks that looked like they'd had been removed from its owner. The fella in the caboose lunged out the window in amazement and probably wondered what happened to create such a sight. For several yards down the tracks we saw him looking back at Rink's cheeks, mooning him. When quiet returned, we were all laughing uproariously. Everyone was yelling, high five slapping, and shoving each other. This was the greatest day of my summer, the absolute greatest.

Chapter Nine: Come Out and Play

Several days passed since the great Rink's Rump trick. I still smiled about it and could only imagine what the guy in the caboose must have thought. My imagination ran wild as I pictured some wise guy, a hunter in the woods, maybe taking a potshot at Rink's bare ass. I was daydreaming while drawing with a piece of white chalk on the smooth cement in the back yard. The old man had decided to cover the trap doors that led down to the basement from the outside. He removed the casing, supports, and the doors, and replaced the works with more support for the cement. When the job was completed, we had an extension to the sitting area where he and ma would sit and drink. He drank his bottle of Jim Beam and she drank her case of beer outdoors every night during the summer.

I remember thinking how kind it was of Rink, giving me the small box of eight pieces of chalk, his payment from Mrs. Reynolds for mowing her yard. He said he could care less about drawing and knew that I tinkered a bit with art. So he passed the box on to me. The smile on my face and the calm inside were interrupted by the sting and ringing in my right ear.

I had not heard Bushy come out of the back door but soon felt a terrible burn on the entire side of my head from his open palm slap. If that wasn't punishment enough, he then squeezed my earlobe and twisted it, twisted it again as if trying to wind up a toy. I yelled in pain as he jerked me up from my drawings of boats on the river. My sisters stopped jumping rope, and my younger brother quit pushing the rotary mower over by the clothesline. There was silence, I guess. All I could hear was the ringing in my ears.

Kicking and flinching, I tried to break his lock on my ear lobe, but the hands of an eight-year-old are no matches for the hardened, muscular grip of a machinist. I think he was cussing as always, but I wasn't certain for I couldn't hear. He ripped and pulled me through the house, and I was running as fast as I could to keep up so as not to have my ear dislodged from the side of my head. Up the stairs we went, and I knew for certain a belt whipping awaited me. He threw me down on my bed and screamed about ruining his cement job with my chalk. I was told, "No supper!"

The last thing I remember was my father growling through clenched teeth, "Quit that goddamn crying, or I'll give you something to cry about!"

The next morning, I awoke to a pain in my upper left rib cage. I thought I was dreaming. "Get up and come with me!" Dad said as he jabbed his index finger into the left side of my chest. He pulled the covers off, and I was startled when I realized it was morning, and I had slept all night without waking once. I also was embarrassed because of my tiny erection. It's perfectly normal for young boys to have an early morning erection when they have to pee. I tried covering myself with my hands the best I could as we pranced past Ma, my mother who had surely seen and heard it all, was sitting on the side of her bed smoking. She didn't say a word, just sat still looking down at the floor and puffing away.

"Get down those goddamn steps right now!" he hollered and gave me a shove.

Please not another beating, please.

He took me around the house to the second room of the 150-year-old basement lined with limestone. He flung out his right arm in the darkness and found the chain for the 40-watt light bulb that provided more shadows than actual illumination. There, at the far end of the cellar, was the doorway hiding the steps that once led up to the backyard and was now entombed with the new patio cement.

"Get your ass in there and do not come out until I tell you to. Do you understand me?" he yelled.

I just nodded my head, and the last thing he said before closing the door was, "You're not mine, and that's why I enjoy doing this shit to you."

The metal latch locked me in and quickly the shadows were replaced with darkness. Total darkness. *What did he mean I'm not his,* I wondered. Moments later I could hear his car start off in the distance. It was about 7:30 in the morning.

The terrible urge to pee was overwhelming. I had no choice but to stand bent over so I didn't hit my head in the cramped stairway that led to nowhere. I smelled the urine and heard it splatter on the dirt below. I didn't care, as I felt such relief. Gradually there were muffled footsteps above as my brothers and sisters began the day and readied themselves to play down at Audubon. I thought for a moment that I smelled toast, and I remembered how I had not eaten since lunch the day before. I was so hungry, but the darkness covered me, and I hid from it the best I could.

Some kind of bug ran across my leg, and I yelled in fright, swatting at my calf, only to miss whatever it was. Our house was filled with *water* bugs as Ma liked to call them. They were in fact cockroaches that would come out in the night, only to scamper under the baseboards when a light was turned on. She would say only people who are filthy have cockroaches and we were not filthy. So we called them water bugs. They ranged from three to five inches long, and if with luck, we stepped on one, the crunching of their hard black shell could be heard across the room. The yellow and purple guts had to be wiped immediately from the linoleum floor, or an ugly stain remained.

Shit, I hope that wasn't a water bug on my leg, I thought as I rubbed my calf. The cool of the cellar was gradually replaced with heat from what I imagined was the rising sun. As time ticked by, sweat dripped from my hair onto my nose and I periodically blew drops off with a quick puff of air from pursed lips. I played a game to see if I could shoot the beads from my nose and hit the slatted door some three feet in front of me. Most would miss and I could hear them crash onto the dirt below. Something would hit my leg and scare me at first, as I figured it was another bug.

Many hours later the dull, cramping pain from the edge of the step against my back forced me to twist and bow and then lean forward to relieve the pressure. There was not a single comfortable position to be had. My eyes seemed to acclimate to the darkness and there were times when I thought I could see light. I held myself in total stillness as I felt a spider crawl on my right shoulder. I wondered where he was heading and felt how lucky he was to be on a mission and probably escape from this place. The bugs no longer frightened me as they brought a diversion. The spider was no different. As I stood perfectly still, he crawled over my shoulder to the outside of my upper arm and stopped. He just sat there. I thought I felt him rubbing his legs together and then he again began the journey down towards my hand. His legs tickled the skin between my fingers, and it was all I could do not to move. Then he was gone. God, it was hot!

I craned my neck and twisted my good ear toward the slats. I thought for a moment I could hear someone calling me. I sat still and wished my pounding heart and dripping sweat would stop, so I could zone in on something, anything.

"Kraaaame. Kraaaame. Come out and play," I heard off in the distance.

Yes, I could hear my best friend, Bear, outside yelling for me to come out and play. Through the eight-inch by twelve-inch cellar window, his voice pierced the darkness and through the wooden barricade, into my ear. What a relief it was! I wasn't abandoned. I wasn't forgotten. I mattered to someone. I felt good in my heart and the tears mixed with the other moisture on my face. I could picture him on the sidewalk above, tossing his head and fixing his glasses.

Then his voice was gone and I was alone again. The hours turned to what seemed like days. I felt every pulse, heard every swallow, and almost heard each muscle move as my aching body screamed for release from this prison. Still, Bushy's words rang through me: *"Do not come out of here!"*

I was hungry. I was thirsty. The noises heard from my siblings earlier had long been replaced with silence, other than Ma's periodic coughing while she must have been watching her soap operas. The television was just too muffled for me to make out what was playing. Again, I drifted off on the vice-like steps, and I must have fallen asleep. The last thing I remember was the heat. God, it was so hot.

With no way to gauge time, I was startled from my sleep when Bushy unlocked the barricade. I had fallen asleep leaning against the dirt wall and it took great effort to stand erect, as he demanded that I come out. I covered my eyes from the bright light ten feet away.

"Now get your ass back up to your bed. Do not talk to anyone. Do not do a thing. Just walk your ass up those stairs," he demanded.

My god! It's dark outside, I thought. What time could it be?

I saw the clock on the stove, and it was ten p.m. Jesus, I had been in that hateful space since 7:30 this morning. Dying for water, I told him I had to take a piss and he waited at the door. I cupped my hands under the water and sucked as much as I could before he slapped me again and told me to go back upstairs to bed.

Before lying down on my bed, I pressed my nose to the screen and smelled the dirt and dust on the tiny squares of metal. I smelled the pleasing aroma of freedom from the packinghouse and heard the animals bellowing for mercy before being slaughtered.

I made a promise to my soul that night, that someday, *someday*, I would get out of here and never come back. I promised myself I would work as hard as I could to be the fastest sprinter in our town, and that would somehow open doors for me. I promised myself that no one, under any circumstances, would ever, ever hurt me again. And with that promise, I made another: I would always get even. And then I remember asking myself as I fell asleep what had he meant when he'd said, "You're not mine, and that's why I enjoy doing this shit to you!"

Chapter Ten: Thy Rod and Thy Staff They Comfort Me

The next day, I wound up at Bear's house. Bushy made me feel like I had to slink around corners but here, in this loving house, I felt safe. "Hey, Twink. What ya up to?" Mac said from the glider on his front porch, as he swung back and forth.

"Awe, nothing much. Where's Bear?"

"Oh, he's up on the can. Speaking of the can, pull my finger," he said, adjusting his glasses as he stuck out his finger.

I knew what was about to happen, but it offered laughter no matter how many times this silly stunt was performed. As I pulled his finger, a ripping fart exploded on the vinyl cushion, a noise that could be heard from across the street. I laughed as he said it was a good one. Mac always made us kids laugh.

In fact, it was from Bear's dad, Mac that we learned how to light farts. On one occasion Bear jumped up, ripped off his pressed jeans, and stood in his white underwear with his new white athletic socks ending just below his skinny calves. Mac handed him the Zippo lighter he'd had since WWII. Bear lifted one leg, popped open the lighter with two fingers as he was taught by Mac, and ignited the flame. Caution was laid to the wind, literally, as he was in a frantic hurry, and he held the flame next to his butt cheeks. I had already turned the lights off and, Boom! There, before us, was the most beautiful orange and red flame shooting all the way to his ankles. The best part was that for just a moment, the flames burned off all the fuzz on his new socks, and they too glowed in the dark.

In addition to lighting farts, there was another tradition at Bear's house. Every Sunday evening at about seven o'clock, we'd order Pusateri's Pizza. We'd wait five minutes or so, then Bear and I would walk up the street to the Lucky Spot Tavern for two six packs of Pepsi. We didn't mind the walk, as it gave us time to smoke. About the time we returned, Pusateri would call back, wanting to confirm it was a real order and not some prank by little kids. Mac would always answer the phone by saying one of two things.

"Stinky's Fish Market. Stinky speaking," or "City Morgue, you stab 'em, we slab 'em."

All of us would howl with laughter, and Mrs. Berry always said the same thing with a giggle, "Oh, Mac."

I knew only one thing about these times: I enjoyed the peace and consistency of it all more than I could say.

"Hey, Twink," Bear said as he came out on the porch. "Where the heck were you yesterday? I came by and called and called, but you never came out."

"Oh, I was busy," I said, trying to change the subject. "Hey, let's get the guys and go to the Pack? There's nothing else to do."

"What the heck are all those bites on your legs and shoulders?" he asked as he pulled me forward from the glider to get a closer look.

"Oh, yeah. Chiggers, I guess," I said, trying to hide the cellar bug bites.

I edged away from him, not so he'd notice, but enough to escape his prying eyes. "So, what do ya think? Do ya want to go?"

"Yep, that'd be fun," Bear said, grinning from ear to ear. "Let's go!"

"You two be careful," Mac called out from as we ran off down the steps.

Going to the Pack was one activity none of our parents minded. Maybe they figured it'd be good for us to see where we'd probably wind up working someday. Farmers would come from three states and hundreds of miles away each day with row after row of livestock trucks. Stinking trucks filled with bellowing cows or snorting pigs. From fancy four-level rigs that could hold a couple hundred pigs, to dilapidated, old rust buckets with wooden slats, these animal haulers had two things in common. Each passed through our neighborhood, and each left behind a stink that made outsiders passing through hold their noses. We grew up with the smell and never gave it a concern.

"Hey, look! There goes another one," Bear yelled, pointing at a truck with Wisconsin license plates as it dropped cakes of straw held together with steaming cow shit.

The bouncing of the tracks jiggled two different kinds of shit loose from the floors of the trucks, only to be run over by the rear tires. Every crossing in our little nest in the city had layered shit ground into the streets on either side.

"Okay, youse guys," Rink bragged. "I'm gonna win today; I am not falling off all the way there," Are youse ready to walk the plank? The first one to fall is a Jap."

Walking the plank was a game everyone played whenever we were walking the tracks. We would separate far enough apart so one person wouldn't affect the success or failure of another. It took laser concentration, agility like a high jumper, and leg strength like an ant that could lift eight times its body weight. Whoever lost was given some disgusting name for about ten seconds and then the talk changed. Today we were about to call someone a dirty Jap, just as our dads said every day.

Blackie took the lead and was some twenty yards in front. He turned to look back. "How are you fuckers doing back there?"

"Okay," Bear yelled.

"I haven't fallen off yet," said Rink.

"Bringing up the rear, and I haven't missed a step," I lied.

The one advantage about being last was that if I fell off, nobody knew about it. I could just step right back on. This way I controlled the game and controlled who won. If I was in a giving mood, I might fake a fall and allow someone else to win after I'd already slipped and fallen two or three times. I had to admit there was something sweet about being in control.

Indeed, Rink won that day, and Blackie lost. So we all called him a Jap three times and punched him in the arm. I was glad Rink won that day. He was a good kid who always helped others, especially those smaller than him. That meant about everybody in our age group.

We finished the three-block contest of walking the tracks and were at the border of the Pack. We ran to the back of the two-block long building to where the most action was. For some strange reason, I felt extra excited and bloody-minded that day. There were dozens of refrigerator trucks lined up at the docks being loaded with full frozen carcasses. Blackie stopped to wave to his dad who was carrying half a cow. He never acknowledged Blackie, and I thought, *what a prick.*

Watching the livestock trucks being unloaded was a ritual of excitement for boys our age. We wandered the area and found ourselves peering through the red metal bars separating us from the animals. The workers ignored us as we pressed our faces to the shit-covered bars; they were too busy whistling, yelling, and slapping the backs and butts of unsuspecting animals that would then jump and push those ahead further down the line.

"Just like home huh, Blackie?" I taunted.

"Awe, fuck you. Besides, Ma's strap is a lot bigger than those. Oh fuck, did ya see that one jump on the back of the other? Do ya think they know what's coming? I wonder what it's like to know when you are about to die," he said, looking straight ahead as if speaking to no one.

Bear and I just looked at each other, did not say a word, and returned to the action. There were more snaps and cracks, jumping and shitting and short-distance charges as they moved toward the scales for weigh-in. The last worker latched the pen shut and after all the animals were weighed, the truck driver was given a slip of paper, and off he went to the office. This process was repeated twenty-four hours a day, seven days a week, all year long, except for Good Friday, Easter, and Christmas.

After being gassed into semi-unconsciousness, the hogs were placed on a conveyor, lying on their sides. Two workers alternated the hog killing by raising an ear and shoving a two-foot steel rod into the brain.

"Hey see that rod in the head?" Rink asked. "It's sorta like what Father Murphy said about a rod and staff, they comfort me," he said as we crouched down to watch through the dirty windows caked with shit and dried blood. We all ignored him, as we were too busy watching. Suddenly, all four legs of another hog gave out a violent quiver after having his brain stuck with the rod. The hog entered the silence of death, and blood poured out of the puncture wound, onto the floor below.

Thirty feet away, cows were hung by their hind legs, hooked to a conveyor, and moved slowly up the line, bellowing in fright and throwing lines of snot on everything nearby. Each cow's head was grabbed by the ear and lifted and twisted to the side. Then, using a razor-sharp knife, life was gone in an instant, as the wound opened from ear to ear.

"Ugh, did you see that?" I yelled to the others.

Nobody heard me over all the dying that was happening beneath us. My favorite part had just happened. Dressed in a yellow plastic apron and wearing black boots, the worker on the far left lifted the cow's head by the ear just as it was giving out a long, last "moo". He literally stopped it in mid-moo, as blood sprayed the walls. The part I did not like much was the ear twisting. It gave me a bad feeling.

Out slid the cow's tongue, as the direction of the blood went from spraying to running, and then just a trickle from the nose and what was once a throat. This area of the Pack was known as the kill section. Conveyors separated the animals, cows went one way, and hogs the other, just like real life in the barnyard.

Workers would slide wooden rods through the hind tendons of the hogs, leaving their lifeless heads dangling in the air. In one five-hour period, 3,000 hogs could be taken from weigh-in to the cooler, after many stops in between.

The hogs were dipped in vats filled with hot liquid tar. Workers donning black rubber gloves and yellow aprons quickly pulled the gooey mess from the carcass, taking most of the hair with it. Then they dropped the tar back into the vat for re-melting. Other workers wearing steel mesh gloves and sharpening steels on their hips would step into the arena of death, scraping off any remaining hair with the knives they carried and sharpened frequently.

Further down the line, one belly after another was cut open with a chainsaw connected to the ceiling with a chain. Blood would pour and squirt on workers, the equipment and the floor. The carcass's heads were cut off and thrown onto a stainless steel table where more than a dozen men waited to cut and peel skin and meat from each cranium.

Digging a thumb into each eye socket, the next worker held the removed head under an automatic cleaver that would proceed to slice the head in halves. He then flipped the appendage to the next person who, using long tweezers, picked out the pituitary gland, a useful scientific part of the pig used in some type of medicine. The next person removed the brains and threw them into a stainless steel tray and they were carted off to the cooler. The head was thrown into a large vat and dumped down a chute for the inedible steamer where it was boiled and processed into dog and cat food products.

Back on the line, six or seven men stood at the ready to remove the inside fat with scrapers. The globs of fat fell like melting snow off a steep roof in springtime. The fat was also sent to inedible. Like skilled surgeons, two additional employees held the entire gut region with one hand, and with a couple of swift slices, removed all the guts and immediately dropped the insides to waiting workers below. Each person was responsible for a separate body part. Lungs, livers, hearts and kidneys soon disappeared from the table.

Finally, the intestines were thrown to a lone worker at the end of the line. He'd cut open an end and slide the shit-filled vessel onto a pipe spraying water. Then, using a back and forth motion, he would work the shit out, spraying anything and anybody nearby, including himself. The intestine was used as casing for sausage. During this entire process the "line" as it was called, never stopped unless a mechanical breakdown occurred. The line ascended to the second floor where the USDA "Seal of Approval" was stamped on the ribs and hams before they got shoved into the cooler.

Workers at the Pack were divided into two groups. One group included college students who worked part time from five pm to ten pm to pay their tuition. The other group included lifers, union members, who worked the same station doing the same job for thirty years. There wasn't any particular resentment between the two groups—it was just the people on one side who had plans to move on, and the people on the other who no longer had any such plans. Many of our parents worked there. Little did I know that ten years down the line I'd be working there myself, spraying the shit out of intestines, pulling brains out of skulls, stamping hog parts with the USDA stamp. It's how I paid for my undergraduate education.

"Okay, I'm f'ing bored," Blackie said, as we all agreed, despite the great killing action.

"Hey, my dad bought me a BB gun. Should we go shoot bums off the box cars again?" Bear asked.

"Naw, not me, I'm going home to lift weights, and then I have to go to Mass," Rink said.

"Holy crap, I'm glad I'm not Catholic," I said, putting a hand to my heart. And thus, guilt-free, I agreed we should shoot some bums.

Blackie clasped his hands under his chin. "Oh, Rink, you" he snipped. "Why can't you miss Mass just once?"

"That's a sin, what youse just said, and now ya have to tell Father next time at confession," Rink replied.

"Oh, screw him," Blackie retorted.

And with a verbal draw, Rink disappeared down the tracks with Bear as Blackie and I assumed our positions down by the hill from Garfield Avenue, over by the round house. We were out of smokes but still had matches I had stolen earlier that day from Sacred Heart. We broke off weeds filled with some type of cream-colored stick stuff. We laid back in the tall weeds and grass and each lit what we called our smokes. Mine burnt my throat as I inhaled, just lying there looking up at the fast-floating clouds, wondering for certain how I'd ever get out of there and *never* return. Neither of us spoke. I wondered what Blackie was thinking, whether he was thinking the same thing, but neither of us dared tell the other.

Chapter Eleven: Fritz's Fence

About twenty minutes later, Bear came walking up with a Daisy 15-shot BB gun his dad had bought for him from Walsh's Department Store on Central Avenue. Blackie and I admired it and told Bear how lucky he was.

"My parents would never buy me something this fucking nice. And if they did, I'd probably shoot 'em," Blackie said, clenching his teeth.

Bear showed us how to load it with those little copper round shots that rattled as we slid them down the chamber. Unused to the pumping action, and the pressure on our shoulders, our arms twisted and quivered as we got to the tenth pump needed to create enough force to eject the projectile some fifty feet away.

"Are ya ready?" I asked, as we started our crawl down the hill through the weeds toward the waiting boxcars.

We were like soldiers, similar to some of the parents in our neighborhood from who'd fought in the War a dozen years prior. We weren't after Japs this time. We were after bums. About three weeks ago one came to my house begging for food. Ma gave him some tomatoes from the garden. I remember peeking around her cotton dress and through the open door as he threw them onto the sidewalk and mumbled something about not liking tomatoes.

Ma shut the door and said, "All right, that's it. I'll never give another thing to those nasty people."

I figured that opened the hunting season, and she would have been proud of me for shooting them.

"Can you guys even see through this tall grass?" Bear asked, as we crawled on our bellies, inching ever so close to the tracks lined with boxcars, many with open, inviting doors.

"Shut the fuck up, Bear. I know it's your gun, but be quiet," Blackie whispered. "We'll never get one in our sights if he hears us."

"Oh, god, this is great," I hissed. "We get to shoot an adult even if he can kick our asses. I know I can out run him."

There was a ditch some ten feet away from an open boxcar. It was covered with grass and weeds at least fifteen feet high, and the ditch itself could have contained seven or eight of us. And so, we laid in wait.

The sound of coughing, hacking, and spitting rose in the air and a minute later, a bum came stumbling up the tracks. Then we heard the smashing of a bottle, which proceeded to break into a million pieces on the rail. We watched the uncertain footing of the drunken bum pass right next to us and he slipped and staggered on the track's rock beds. Then he started singing.

"I've been working on the railroad, all the live long days," he warbled, choking on the words or his own spit. He turned, and hacked a goober into the weeds. It dripped off the grass and onto Blackie's left cheek.

The bum caught sight of us, observed the gun and threw out a few choice words. "Give me that dirty, fucking gun right now! That fucker's all mine, right in the eyes."

Little did that unfortunate tramp realize that he had, unknowingly, released the fury of eight years of abuse suffered from the hands of adults who'd turned their progeny into one of the meanest, most disrespectful kids in our neighborhood. All from one good hocker. I looked over at Blackie who already had the bum, now seated bum in the open boxcar, in his sights. He mumbled a few cuss words under his breath and squeezed.

"Eiyeee" the guy screeched and fell back, holding his left eye. A direct hit!

Blackie was already pumping number nine, and then ten, as he stood and ran toward the open car.

"Give me my gun!" Bear yelled. "Let's get the heck out of here. You really hurt him!"

The pain-stricken bum didn't see Blackie standing over him inside the car. He was too busy screaming.

"Take this too, you son of a bitch!" Blackie screamed as the fella looked up.

I heard another pop, and the first scream was mute compared to this one. Blood was now coming out of both eyes. He cupped his filthy hands over the sockets that once allowed sight. This guy was rolling in the rail car, screaming so loudly the cars were slowing down on the street above to see what was happening. The railroad dick was alerted from the guardhouse and was on the run to the open car to see what had happened.

"Blackie, get the hell out of there!" I screamed. "A railroad dick's coming up the tracks!" I screamed and ran faster than ever run before.

Blackie jumped and then rolled onto the gravel with the railroad cop just steps away. Blackie jumped the ditch and scurried up the hill, carrying the gun and yelling back at the shithead who'd had spit on him. Never mind that it was accidental.

I passed Bear who had a two-block lead, and we all separated off in different directions. Bear went up the alley towards Rugenitz's Drug Store while Blackie cut down the opposite alley towards Merle the janitor's house. Because I didn't know where else to go, I ran straight for Huey's. Out of air and breathing hard, I came to a halt against the three-foot limestone wall across from the store. I kept looking to my left to see if anyone was coming, but the coast was clear.

An old blue Buick was parked in front of Huey's store with its trunk open. I watched the Duncan Yoyo salesman demonstrating "walking the baby" to a large group of little kids. And for some reason, the sight was sad as they each peered over the other to get a good view. And I couldn't help but think, a Duncan yoyo today, and a Daisy 15-shot BB gun tomorrow.

It seemed like an eternity before I caught my wind and could breathe easily again. I paid little attention to the ten or twelve kids watching the yo-yo demonstration. My legs felt weak, as I tried to swallow the truth. *Blackie had really hurt that guy, and we could all be in big trouble.*

A minute or so later, Rink came running up East 22nd Street, probably on his way to mass or confession "Hi ya, Krame," he hollered.

I didn't acknowledge him. I just looked and wondered what it felt like to help others in the neighborhood, rather than going off with us, doing what we all did. Off in the distance I heard an ambulance over by Garfield Avenue.

The next evening at about eight o'clock, we were watching Gunsmoke and I got thirsty. During a commercial, I went to the kitchen for a drink of water. I hadn't seen any of my friends, as I was too scared to be around anyone. Ma told me to get her another Hamm's beer from the fridge when I went out to the kitchen. Ma never asked, she just told. I stalled for few minutes, rattling the bottles against each other, taking my time, worry filling my chest like a helium balloon. As I passed ma, I put the beer on the table beside her.

Suddenly, Bushy growled. "Did you or any of your hoodlum friends have anything to do with hurting the bum over by Garfield yesterday?"

I felt as if I'd been knocked against the wall, yet I straightened my shoulders and tried to look innocent. "What do you mean? I haven't been over there in a long time. What happened?"

He put down his newspaper on the side table and said something about a bum being shot by kids and how he'd been blinded in one eye. When he lifted his glass to take another drink, his mixed drink of Squirt and Jim Beam pulled the paper from the table as it sweated in the hot summer night. He pushed the newspaper from the bottom of his drink and took another deep swig. "You better not be lying to me, or you won't be able to sit for a month when I'm done with you!"

I forgot all about my water and the TV show. I gave Ma another beer and went up to my bedroom, which was nothing more than a bed in the narrow hallway next to a window. I had to walk sideways between the railway over the steps and the bed itself to lie down. I sat on my bed hearing the animals at the pack on their way to death. I whispered a promise to myself, "Someday, I will get out of here and never come back."

A few days later I was sitting on the front steps, inches from the sidewalk watching cars pass up and down the street. My boredom was interrupted from the smoke coming from our neighbor's backyard. I edged down the narrow path between his house and ours; the two houses a mere three feet apart. I turned sideways to pass the window air conditioner that hung out of our kitchen window. Our neighbor, Fritz was busy smoking carp. He'd built a smoker from cement blocks that were covered on top with a piece of tin. It was common knowledge that the only way to eat carp was to eat it smoked. Fritz was a huge man with a heavy German accent, a sort of guttural accent that was difficult to understand yet fun to hear. I understood only half of what he said. He was a kind man, just like Huey. He never gave me a cross word and always wanted to know what I'd been doing. I told him about the first-place blue ribbons I'd won last week while running sprints, representing Audubon School Playground in the All-City track meet.

"Oh yea, I sawed how youse can run really quick when de old man Kupperschmidt come after youse with his gun when youse stole apples off him tree last week. Youse was the last to leave the yard and passed all de udders by da time youse was near my house. My gross papa was a quick runner like you in de ole country. Youse remind me of him."

One minute, I was sitting there listening to Fritz, and the next, I was being torn from my perch on the fence, my hands burning like hot ashes. Earlier I'd climbed to the top square of the chicken wire fence so I could look Fritz in the eye. It was his fence and he never seemed to mind. But it sure enough had pissed off Bushy, the ever-present, all-knowing Bushy.

My fingers were still stinging when I heard the old man say, "Goddammit! How many times have I told you not to climb on that fence? Get your ass upstairs. I'll be right up."

Already crying, I looked back at Fritz for some redemption and he turned to check the carp. I cried louder as I went inside, hoping Ma would save me. She said nothing as she put her beer on the table and I heard her belch as I rounded the steps, crying even louder. Here it was: two additional adults who had not saved me or protected me. That fucking bum deserves what he got from Blackie, I thought. That's how little I knew.

I heard dad in the distance and then I heard him taking the steps two at a time. I heard the slap of his belt being removed. I was begging for mercy and crying so loud all the neighbors must have heard me, and yet none came to my rescue. He shoved me to the floor so he could get a long swing and pulverized me not with the belt, but with the buckle. My fingers no longer hurt from being ripped off the fence. Now it was the pain of chunks of skin being torn away from my forearm as I protected my face. My ribs cracked as I felt his work boot hit me. I stopped crying instantly. I could not breathe. I lay curled in a ball and didn't give a damn what happened next.

Nothing happened. Just more of the same; I knew it was to bed and again no supper. That was fine with me. As I learned quickly, I was my own best friend, and there was no one in the world that could protect me. I hated Fritz. I trusted nobody, not a soul to help me ever again.

An hour or so later, I was awakened by Mark who told me we were all going for ice cream. I bolted out of bed and didn't feel any more pain. Often this would happen where I'd be punished and then later we might get some kind of reward. Tonight it was ice cream. Bushy was back in a good mood and didn't say a cross word all the way to the Cone House a few blocks away from Fulton School. I ordered my favorite – strawberry - and we were all allowed to get two scoops. Bushy ordered butter brickle. We sat outside the place on the wrought iron chairs watching traffic pass by, licking our cones, savoring the last bites. Despite the fact that my life was a cycle of punishment, then reward, that afternoon sure was a good time.

Chapter Twelve: The Limp

I ran along the sidewalk triumphantly, slamming the scuffed baseball into my dusty glove. I was thinking how hot it was but that didn't matter as we'd just won another game at Audubon. It was terrific, that game because those of us from Audubon had played those Catholics from Sacred Heart. I turned the corner onto Lincoln to the sight of my dad leaning into the opened hood of our car. Once again the old rust bucket wouldn't run.

"Hi, Dad," I said as I walked past, expecting no response.

He looked up, and reached for another tool. "Hi, Krame. How was the game?"

"Problems with the car again, huh?"

"Now what the Judas Priest does it look like I'm doing here?" he snapped from beneath the hood. "Do you think I have nothing better to do?"

I said nothing but walked into the house, set my ball and glove on the coffee table and picked up the latest edition of *Boys' Life*. While I was trying to solve the monthly puzzle, I heard him yelling.

"Goddamn you son of a bitch! I said to stop when I gave you a wave."

I climbed up on the back of the davenport to look out the window to see who he was yelling at now.

"Get your ass in the house. You're not good for a thing you son of a bitch. Send your sister out here now," he continued, his voice rising with every word.

I watched Mark climb out of the front seat from behind the steering wheel. I hadn't noticed him when I'd passed by moments earlier. I knew immediately what had happened. Whichever kid was behind the wheel had to try and start the engine when Bushy thought it was fixed. Dad expected us to stop as soon as he waved his hand.

Mark rushed into the house, bawling.

"What's the matter with you now?" Ma asked as she blew smoke from her L&M cigarette. She was sitting at the kitchen table watching the Cubs game on WGN.

"Dad yelled at me again and said I was good for nothing. He wants Maggie to go help now," Mark said between sobs.

"Well, maybe you aren't good for nothing sometimes, did you ever think of that? You have to learn to pay attention and... oh, wow! A standing double by Martinez!" She stopped in mid-sentence to return to watching her ball game.

Mark walked past me and I pretended not to notice a thing. It was his battle, and each of us kids learned early on not to get involved. He went upstairs, and I heard the crying subside. In a few minutes, the sound of clicking and squeaking wafted down the stairs. I knew what Mark was doing. He had opened his viola case and was tuning the instrument. He began playing, and I knew all was right with him.

The Dubuque School System offered a free program in all the elementary schools where children could choose any instrument and use it for free while learning to play. I'd tried the violin last year but in frustration had slammed it against the dresser. I couldn't even play my scales! Ma and dad had to buy a new one to replace the one I'd shattered that day. The whipping I got was nothing compared to the satisfaction I felt in destroying that damn thing.

"Ah-ha, Trigger," I said aloud as I figured out the name of Roy Rogers' horse and wrote it into the crossword puzzle at nine down.

"Pow, boom, choke, and sputter" came from the street outside as Maggie turned the ignition key. I was on the back of the davenport again looking out at the excitement as dad slammed the hood. "Okay, we got it. Just let it idle. Great job, Maggie. Thanks for your help, you did great," he said as he gave her a big hug and then bent over to pick up his sockets and wrenches.

From upstairs the music quit, and I imagined Mark also watching out the window. He came down the stairs, and in a sarcastic tone that imitated Dad, said under his breath, "Good job, way to go. Piss on you, you son of a bitch." Mark's music had once again worked its magic and he was in a better mood. Nonchalantly, he went to the kitchen to see how the Cubs were doing.

Dad's house rule meant he never hit the girls, as only a weakling would assault a female, no matter the age. While it did breed resentment among us boys, looking back, it was a good rule. Boys, on the other hand, were fair game.

I returned to my puzzle when he came in and yelled at me, "Goddamn you! How many times have I told you never to put your glove and ball on the coffee table? Now I'll show you what happens when you don't listen." He picked up my ball and glove and threw it into the bathroom garbage basket. "How do you like that?"

I was silent, since I was two steps ahead of him. It was my week to empty all the trash, and I already knew where I'd would hide it in the garage after pretending to dump it in the trash cans out in the alley.

"Did you get the car started?" Ma asked.

"Yeah, it runs great. I sure do feel good. Hey Mark, ask Krame if the two of you want to go up to the dam and watch the barges go through."

"Okay, that'll be great, Dad," Mark said, accustomed to Dad's abrupt change of moods.

Some fifteen minutes later, we were approaching the grand arches the elm trees created when they met in the middle of Rhomberg Avenue from either side of the street. It was like a tunnel made by Nature and lasted a good two blocks. Years later, these majestic trees would all be removed because of Dutch Elm Disease. But now, here they stood, a regular part of my childhood. I was too young I guess to be properly grateful.

"Hey, look. We're just in time," Bushy said as he parked the car, and we scrambled out.

A tugboat was pushing three long barges full of coal, waiting for the lower lock to open. There was a safety fence, supposedly, that kept visitors from getting too close and falling in. It couldn't have been a very strong fence since the weight of the three of us nearly bent it in half. I wondered what the difference was from this fence and the one that separated our yard from Fritz's yard? I was always wondering about stuff like that and spent a lot of time in my head, which for the most part, was a safer place to be.

The water level dropped past each foot marker painted on the walls of the lock and eventually a very loud horn would sound from the station and a return horn from the tug sounded back. The gates slowly opened and the barges moved into place. Workers were busy running back and forth, attaching heavy ropes to four-foot diameter cement plugs used to tie it off temporarily.

Dad cupped his hands around his mouth and yelled to a worker "Hey, where did you start and where are you headed?"

"We came out of St. Louis and are going up to St. Paul," the guy yelled back.

We watched for over an hour until the tug and barges were just memories and had disappeared up river. Walking back to the car, I was filled with excitement at what the three of us had experienced. A real father/son experience! Carelessly, I tripped on a broken piece of sidewalk.

I felt the smack on the side of my face as I righted myself and managed to catch my balance. "You stupid klutz," Dad said as he slapped me.

It didn't bother me a bit as I was thinking about maybe riding a barge to some far off place someday, somewhere far away from here. We turned onto Lincoln Avenue, and he said, "Now who the hell has my parking spot?"

Finding a place to park on the narrow street often provided a reason for any resident to let out a string of cuss words. In the winter, when there was even less room because of the snow banks, there was a lot of cussing going on by motorists trying to get by parked cars and those attempting to get close to what was actually a curb in other seasons.

Right away, I recognized the Blackhawk County, Iowa, license tag and knew it was Uncle Matt's car. He and Aunt Karen were here to visit and I felt a sudden burst of happiness. Uncle Matt was dad's younger brother who still lived in Cedar Falls, where dad grew up. He and Grandpa Kramer worked at the same plant called Clay Manufacturing. Grandpa could walk to work as the plant was just across the street from his house. Dad really liked Uncle Matt and his other brother, Rex. However, he hated his third brother Neal. Apparently Neal was Grandpa's favorite son and had no trouble telling others how he felt.

"What a nice surprise. I'm so glad to see you two," Dad said as he they all shook hands. "Let's have a drink."

Uncle Matt grinned. "Karen and I were bored, so we just got in the car and ended up here. I hope you don't mind if we stay the night."

"Heck no. This is just great. I'm glad you came up," Dad said.

Locking my head and neck with one arm and rubbing the top of my head with a Dutchman's rub was a sign of pure affection and Uncle Matt performed this ritual every time he came to visit. "How's the running coming along? Has anyone ever beat you yet? Do you have any new ribbons to show me, you little rascal?"

I puffed out my chest. "Yeah, I just won another blue ribbon at the All-School Playground track meet held at the high school."

"Good boy, I swear you'll do something great someday with all your speed."

Of all my aunts and uncles, Uncle Matt was my favorite. For years, I had wished he lived closer. Things were always great when he was around. We were never punished in any way whenever he came to town. I was glad they were spending the night: a rare 24 hour period of peace.

"Who won the game?" Mark asked Mom.

"I don't know. I had to turn it off when *they* came in," she said in a stinging tone.

About an hour later I was trying to burn an ant with a magnifying glass I found as a prize in a box of Cracker Jacks. He was a big one with two distinct body parts. I squashed the back part so he couldn't get away. He just lay there struggling while the sun shot a laser-like beam into his head. Dad and Uncle Matt were at the picnic table finishing another beer when Uncle Matt asked Dad, "So how's the foot doing? Giving you any trouble?"

I stopped what I was doing to eavesdrop. I continued to lie on my side and pretend to fry the ant.

"Oh, it bothers me some, especially when I have to walk from one end of the plant to the other. The limp gets real noticeable and then my hip acts up. You know, I'll never forgive dad for not getting help for me right after I was born. He knew the Shriners would help kids with a clubfoot. There are times when I have pain with every step that I cuss him in my mind. I hate that religious son of a bitch. Some kind of god he prays to that allowed his first-born son to crawl for three years and then to hop on a crutch for another three," Dad said as I froze in my tracks.

I always knew he had a limp, and so did all the other kids in the neighborhood. I just figured it was his normal walk and never asked about it. One time Blackie, Bear, Rink and I were hiding at the far end of Audubon playground, lying in the ditch waiting for it to get completely dark. We were going to ring doorbells and then run away. It was nearing dark but not quite, when Bear noticed my dad walking along Johnson Street.

"Hey, look, Krame. There's your dad. I can tell by the way he walks. I can't see all of him 'cause it's getting dark, but he's the only one who walks like that."

A wave of fear washed over me. "Oh shit! Everybody lay low and don't move. If he knows I'm down here he'll come after me."

Just then Blackie gave out a yell, "Hey Bushy, you son of a bitch."

In the twilight I saw him stop and turn toward the four of us. He was a good seventy-five yards away and was bent over at the waist trying to see who was back by the fence. He just stood there bent over for what seemed like an eternity. Finally, he stood back up and continued limping back towards the house.

"Blackie, you goddamn son of a bitch!" I said as I punched him wherever the blows would land. It took the other two to get me off of him and I never did ring doorbells that night because I was so pissed off.

The screen door slammed as dad brought two more beers out for him and Uncle Matt. Uncle Matt took a deep swig. "Yeah, if wasn't for Uncle Preston, god only knows how bad you would have been. The way I heard it from Mother many years ago, Uncle Preston told Dad that as his older brother he was taking you to the Shriners to get your foot fixed, and there was nothing Dad could do about it."

Dad took a long swig of beer. "Yep, that's about right. I was six years old when I could finally walk without a crutch. I'll never forgive Dad. But that's not the worst thing that old bastard did to me." His face flushed an angry red. "I remember him telling me that my foot deformity was a sign from the Devil, who'd mangled his first-born son. Isn't that some shit?"

Uncle Matt swore under his breath. "You know what it is. It's that stupid religious group they have been a part of all their lives. I remember one time when he beat me out in the shop with that razor strap that always hung by the door. And before he did, he said he had two good sons and two bad sons. He said you and I were the bad sons, and it gave him great pleasure to whip us."

Sitting there unobserved, I wondered how it'd feel to be a priest with people telling you shit like that. At least I had two good feet.

"Yea, the best thing that ever happened to me was getting out of there and moving here to Dubuque," Dad said angrily. "And I don't plan on going to the son of a bitch's funeral when he dies."

Uncle Matt put a hand on Dad's shoulder. "Well, at least you have a good family now."

Dad didn't say a word, not one stinking word.

Chapter Thirteen: Cold and Deep

"You idiot!" I heard Bear say to Blackie as I approached the elm tree.

"Awe, fuck. It wasn't my fault. What was I supposed to do with the gun? Huh? If I would of kept it, we would be in jail for blinding that stinking bum. I had to throw it away in that garbage can up the alley." He took a deep breath then started in again. "Besides, I couldn't run nearly as fast as Krame, carrying it. Somebody would have caught me. So there, you fucker! I don't care what Mac says."

Blackie shot him a look. "Just lie to him."

Bear paced back and forth nervously. "What youse guys talking about? Why's everybody so pissed? Oh shit, now I have to tell Father I cussed at my next confession. Boy, will he be mad."

Rink stared at me curiously. "Krame, what happened to your arm? Looks like a Jap got a hold of you."

"Aw, just another run-in with the old man," I replied.

It was the first time we'd all been together since the "bum blinding" as we called it. Mac chewed out Bear for losing his BB gun. Mac said he'd never again buy anything nice for him. Bear told him he left it on the tracks by mistake and some other kids must have picked it up. Little did Mac know that Blackie ditched it in a garbage can in the alley behind Shindler's place. Some lucky garbage collector must have taken it home to his kid and Bear was really pissed off now.

"So what are we doing today?" Rink asked. "I don't have a single chore. Do youse guys want to know what I recorded lifting today with my three older brothers?"

"No!" we shouted, united for a change.

Bear was mad about losing his gun, but Blackie was just mad, just plain no-reason mad.

"Hey, do youse guys want to go and jump off the train bridge?" Rink asked excitedly.

One by one, we looked at each other, and again united in brotherhood, shouted, "Hell yes!"

Together, we had survived hopping a train, blinding a bum, stealing pop bottles from Huey's, stealing a plank from the lumberyard, and many other escapades. All of these adventures had been performed by the age of eight, except for Rink who was nine. It was like we were in a competition with Life.

Alone, I had survived beatings, isolation, humiliation, thirst, starvation and abandonment. No one of any age, *no one* in our neighborhood had ever attempted a jump from the train bridge. No one at any age had experienced what I had. And there was not a person to tell it to. If we didn't break our necks in the process, we'd be heroes to the younger kids, admired by the older ones and respected by our fathers—maybe.

But in an instant, the moment of sheer excitement left me. "Wait a minute. Have you guys given any thought to this? We could get hurt. Well, at least three of us could," I said looking around the group. "Rink can handle anything with his weight lifting. But what happens if the tender catches us? I'll get a beating like no tomorrow. And you, Bear, your dad's already pissed about you losing the gun. Blackie, I don't see any problem with you. But I think we need to plan this. Just like all things, we should never get caught."

Blackie faced me squarely. "Oh fuck you, Krame! And what about not planning when you had us steal that plank from the lumberyard? That all worked out just fine. You even said it was the best day of your life, and with no planning!"

"Yeah, I remember the same thing, Krame," Bear said. "And besides, I can't get in any more trouble than I am already for somebody losing my gun."

I held up both hands, palms forward, warding off their attacks.

Rink grimaced. "Hey, youse guys. I already have to confess to Father about swearing. So what do I care? And besides, it's my idea. I say we just do it."

"Hey, Rink," Blackie said, laughing out loud. "If we do get caught, Krame and I will lie for you and say you weren't with us. We aren't Catholic and don't have to go to confession anyway."

"Yeah, you fucker," Blackie said, joining in. "We'll tell everybody you were off helping some old woman in the neighborhood. Everyone will believe us."

I let out a low whistle. "Yeah, we're so trustworthy, right, guys?

We all laughed and headed for the tracks for our two-mile hike to the East Dubuque train bridge. Blackie furnished the smokes, and I supplied the matches. Our stealing ability had become quite keen, and others depended on us for needed wares. It wasn't Japs this time but Redskins we would call one another when someone fell off the tracks.

We were doing our balancing act down the tracks two blocks from where we started. It was behind Eagles Supermarket that I yelled out, "Hey, and watch out for Mean Boy. He lives just up ahead in the flats."

"Oh, shit I forgot about him," Rink said nervously.

Bear made a 'T' with his two hands. "Time out, time out! Who's Mean Boy, and how come I never heard of him before?"

Blackie hooted. "He's meaner than any of our dads, stronger than Rink, quicker than Krame—well just about."

I stopped and looked back, feeling like the head of the pack. "His name's Mean Boy Menos. He lives up ahead in the Flats beyond the Pack. Do you see where our tracks meet those ten to fifteen other tracks two blocks up ahead where all those broken down cars are on the left? He lives in one of those old wooden houses. I never thought about mentioning him because he stays in his neighborhood and we stay in ours. None of us has ever gone this far before, so it wasn't any big deal."

Bear put his arms across his chest and pretend shivered. "Ooh, we're real scared. But we still don't know why's he called Mean Boy."

Rink balanced himself as he jumped. "Some older kids at the tree said when the kid was six, he would climb up top of the box cars and jump from one to another. One day there was a railroad dick walking along the cars and Mean Boy jumped off the top and snagged himself right around that dick's neck and pulled him to the ground. They said the guy had to hit him four or five times with his Billy club to get him off, and Mean Boy just ran away under the train on all fours like some kind of spider laughing his head off."

"Yeah," Blackie hollered. "And I heard his Ma had to chain him to a tree in their backyard. Seems there was a painter up on the ladder when Mean Boy came around the corner and shook it as hard as he could, trying to knock the guy off. Because of the painter's screaming, Mean Boy's Ma came out and saved the guy. So she chained the kid to a tree." Blackie bent down and picked up an empty beer bottle for protection.

Bear wiped the sweat from his face, pushed his glasses back in place. "What does he look like? How old is he? How will we know when to run?"

Leave it to Bear to get to the essentials, I thought. "None of us has ever seen him. All we know are the stories from older kids. He's our age, I think."

Bear did a double take. "Now wait a minute, if none of you has ever seen him, is he real, or is it a prank by the older kids. You know, like a snipe hunt in Scouts?"

"Two of my older brothers saw him once," Rink said, pointing up the tracks. "See that metal scrap yard up ahead on the right? My brothers came down here last year to buy some heavy pieces of metal they could lift in the back yard, so they didn't have to wait so long taking turns with the weights we have. My dad came back later and loaded it into the truck for them."

"Jesus, get to the point," Blackie interrupted.

"Anyway, they saw him hiding in that tall grass next to the big metal fence. As they turned the corner, there he was with only his head sticking out looking at them." Rink shuddered. "They said he had a huge head that had some kind of bulge on the left side—kinda like when youse get a bulge in your bicycle tire. His right eye was higher than his left, he had wide nostrils and one ear lobe was missing."

"Wow, so that's what they were talking about," I exclaimed. "I remember Bushy telling Fritz about him; that he was so ugly when he was born his mother carried him upside down for the first three days and thought he had only one eye. I remember Fritz laughing at that but I don't get it. I do get the part where he is pretty messed up though."

"Is he retarded or something?" Bear asked.

"Not at all," I replied. "He is exceptionally smart for his age. I heard other adults say he has great sarcasm—whatever that means—and likes to ask people questions just before he attacks."

Bear glanced around anxiously. "So what do we do to get out of here safely? Should we walk the street, go home or what?"

"Fuck no," Blackie yelled. We're turning back and we're *not* going down the street. There are four of us and I say everybody get a weapon. I already have this empty bottle I'll throw right at him. Or better yet, I'll smash it right where his foot is next to the tracks, and it'll break into a million pieces and cut him all over."

One by one, the rest of us scampered around looking for weapons.

Bear yelled out. "Hey look at this! It's a railroad spike. I can stick him right in the heart with it like a vampire killing."

I picked up a chain to go along with my hubcap. "What'd you get, Rink?"

"I got this big stick I'll use to spear him in the guts if he gets too close." He stared at me in disbelief. "What are youse doing with a hub cap?"

"It's a shield in case he throws something at us," I said.

Bear practically growled. "All right then, I'm also getting this big rock to match my spike."

I laughed out loud. "Look at us. We look like those guys on *Demetrius and the Gladiators*. Here's what I think we should do. Blackie, you and Bear watch the right side of the tracks, especially around that tall grass up ahead. Rink, you watch across the tracks by those houses and junk cars. I'll watch our backs." I was so good at this, I should become a traffic cop. "I say we stay on the right and get off the tracks on that path so we can take off running if need be."

"Great idea, Krame," Bear agreed.

While it was only three city blocks, it seemed like miles before we were in the clear and able to drop our makeshift weapons. Each of us was sweating buckets and Bear couldn't see a thing, his glassed were so grime-smeared. We sat on the rail and took a break while Bear wiped his lenses with his shirt. Eventually the Mean Boy episode was far behind us . . . but up ahead lay the *real* adventure for the day.

Everyone in our neighborhood called it the East Dubuque Railroad Bridge, as it connected Dubuque, Iowa, with East Dubuque, Illinois. Now, three eight-year-old kids and one nine-year-old were going to conquer it. We were going to jump off it into the strongest river in the world and swim downstream. We would be remembered forever.

"Hey, read this plaque here by the shot tower," I said as the others came running up the hill.

Bear let out what sounded like a war whoop. "Oh boy. Just think, less than one hundred years ago this thing made cannon balls for the North during the Civil War. And it also made shot for rifles, according to what's written here."

"Who fucking cares?" Blackie sneered, pointing ahead. "Look, there's the bridge right there. I hope you fuckers are ready for a thrill. Any of you chicken out I'll knock your teeth out! Better yet, I'll throw you into my kitchen at home with Ma, who will really knock the shit out of you."

Everybody started shoving and punching one another like they were practicing for Blackie's mom.

"Hey youse guys, come over here and read this," Rink yelled from about fifty yards away where he was standing on the bank of the river.

It was another plaque that told about the bridge. Bear peered closely at the sign, mumbling half aloud while stopping every few words to fix his glasses. "Built in 1869, it was the fifth railroad bridge to cross the Mississippi, built by Andrew Carnegie, cost $800,000, and center section pivots so barges can pass through." Then he said two things none of us had thought about or even considered.

"Goddamn! This bridge is fifty feet above the water! Jesus, this is listed as one of the most powerful waterways in the world! What the hell am I going to do with my glasses? If I lose those as well as my BB gun, my dad really will be pissed!"

"Oh fuck you," Blackie said, forcing a laugh. "Mac won't be pissed off. He'll just buy you another pair. We're already lying for Rink. I guess we can come up with something for you too."

"Okay, Bear," I said, once again regaining control. "Just put your glasses in your pocket. If you wear them, they'll come off for sure, and you can't hold them in your hand 'cause you need those for swimming to the sand bar when we resurface. The way I see it, the worst thing is that they'll break, but you won't lose them," I promised.

"That's what I like about you, Krame. You're are always thinking about not getting caught and stuff," he said. "So how are we going to do this?"

"All right. Here's how I see this," I started while all the others gathered around me. "We know there's a bridge tender half way out there. His job is to sound alarms and open the bridge sideways so barges can come up or down river. First, we make sure there are no barges anywhere around. That means he will be in his shack. Second, there is that lower level for workers with that wide plank below the tracks. I say we crawl across the lower plank until we're way past his shack," I said as the others hung on every word.

"Gees," Bear said, no doubt mirroring the other's thoughts. "How do you know this'll work?"

I leaned in and made strong eye contact. "When the coast is clear, we jump up and run like fuckers, as Blackie would say. When we get up and out over the channel, we jump. We all meet at the sand bar in East Dubuque."

"Who's going first?" Rink asked.

Blackie stepped forward. "Me, you cowards. I was the only one *not* made a Redskin on the walk down the tracks. Krame, you were last on the tracks, so I say you're last here. You other two fuckers can fight over the other spots."

"Fight? Youse guys want to fight? I'll fight everyone," Rink shouted. He thumped his chest. "I can lift more weights, carry more groceries, and push a lawn mower farther than any of youse guys put together."

"No, Rink you go second," Bear replied, folding, and then putting his glasses into the pocket of his shorts.

I nodded in agreement. "I'll be last cause I'm the fastest, in case the tender catches us." I looked around with what I felt as an air of readiness. "One last thing. Stay out of the channel once we come up. Swim for the shore as fast as you guys can. Rink, you are the strongest by far, so you shouldn't have any problem, but the rest of us better push hard for the shore."

Rink liked it that I recognized his strength. He flexed his biceps, like a big-time wrestler, then turned around. After a minor adjustment, he pivoted around facing us with his eyelids turned inside out. "Hey look, youse guys."

We all yelled different things at him, none of which were very kind. He just slapped his thigh, laughed, and said, "Aha, I got youse guys again!"

The first thing I noticed as we hoisted ourselves onto the gangplank was the wind. Twenty feet away, across the street from the shot tower, there wasn't even a breeze, but here the wind was fierce.

The second thing I noticed was the tar! My hands seemed to stick with each small reach and grasp, moving slowly ahead like a cat after some tasty prey. Well, at least, I thought, we won't fall off with all this tar. My knees and hands were sticking like my tongue to a frozen sled runner in winter.

Off to my left I could see the Wisconsin Bridge, the lock and dam, and even the dump, with multiple garbage trucks passing in and out. To my right was the East Dubuque Bridge with cars whizzing back and forth and I wondered where everyone was going in such a hurry. Not an adult in the world could see us four little kids pulling off the greatest trick ever, us waiting there together at the edge of time. If they could see us, they wouldn't care. Nobody cared, not really. But when this was over, we would be legends. And legends never die. We would be the envy of everyone. I pictured in my mind the bigger kids giving us a seat right up against the base of the elm tree at Audubon. I thought about my dad maybe not hitting me anymore because of my daring nature. I thought about Merle the janitor being a little kinder to each of us.

"Wow, oh, god!" I yelled as a gust of wind almost shot me off the gangplank. But nobody heard me, nobody at all. The wind was filling our ears and there was no room for normal sound. I saw Bear trying to push his hair back. A full tube of Brylcreem wouldn't even hold it in place against this zephyr that we were fighting. Suddenly, way ahead I saw Blackie hunker down further than he ever had while stealing pop bottles behind Huey's. Directly behind him, I noticed Rink's muscles contract and relax as he alternated his grip with each forward move. I knew we were approaching the halfway point where the bridge tender's shack was bolted to its base. There was no turning back.

There was no fear inside me, no hesitation, no worries. My sense of serenity and focus were the most keen in my life up to that point. I was proud to be free. I was so happy to be with three of my best friends, each so different, yet we were so close. We were always there for each other, never judging one another, even though we liked to harass and poke fun. I remember watching Blackie way up ahead and feeling proud of him. There were no mother's harsh words or straps against him now. He was a leader at that moment.

Rink was such a nice kid and always did what was right. I thought for a moment how different we were. Then there was Bear, my best friend. I was glad I had met him in Miss Phifner's class, even though he'd interrupted my thoughts about her attractive legs.

More than fifty feet below, I saw what looked like a floating matchstick that I'd stolen from the candle section up front at Sacred Heart Church. Bear saw it at the same time. He twisted just enough not to lose his grip and looked back at me. He bobbed his head downward, as if to point. I acknowledged with a nod of my head. There it was, a plank of wood being pushed down the rumbling current of the river. Even from so high up, it looked like the plank we'd stolen from the lumberyard. I wondered if it dislodged itself from the dam and gradually worked its way here now, heading south, never to be seen by us again. That sure was another great day, the day we stole that plank.

I smiled to myself as I continued to crawl and pull myself further along. This was the best day ever.

"Hey, you sons-a-bitches," I heard as we were up and running across the tracks. "Get the hell back here," the tender screamed as we all were running farther along toward the Illinois side.

I'd been so caught up in the moment I didn't remember even jumping up on to the tracks. His screams brought me back to reality in an instant. The others were out over the channel on the moving part of the bridge, no doubt yelling for me to run.

I saw their lips moving but couldn't hear them. The guy was so close behind me; his cussing and screaming were easy to pick up. I remember smiling to myself and thinking I should change gears. No fucking adult was going to stop me now. I increased both my stride and speed and soon, I left him far behind. I saw all three of my pals jumping as I turned to get square. Rink had a huge grin, Bear looked scared to death and Blackie had a look of determination I'd never seen before. Rink and Blackie each held their noses. Bear clutched his pocket where his glasses waited unaware. As for me, I didn't hesitate as I jumped into the murky water. It was like moving in slow motion, and it seemed like a full day before I finally hit the water.

God, it was cold, so cold and so deep. I could feel my tiny frame being pushed downriver. Exhilaration was replaced with sudden fear. I used every muscle I possessed to pull and twist against the deep current, the power of it sucking me down to the bottom and further along its southern course. I fought its grip just like I fought the grip of my dad with every beating. My dad was stronger because I could never get away from him. But now, here, I shot to the top of the river and sucked in a huge breath! I reached the East Dubuque sand bar some three quarters of a mile from our jump with only two strokes of the American crawl. Immediately, a group of teenagers were running toward all of us and laughing, clapping their hands, and slapping our backs.

One real tall kid with carrot colored hair and a face full of pimples said, "Oh my god, you three sons-a-bitches are crazy. Holy shit!"

Three, had he just say three? I asked myself.

Chapter Fourteen: Pile of Ants

Blackie screamed at me over the roar of the gathering crowd. "Where the fuck is Rink?"

My heart skipped a beat. "You mean he's not here?"

Bear was holding his shattered glasses in his left hand and wiping tears from his eyes with the other. "Where the fuck is he? He's not pulling a trick on us is he? Rink," he yelled as loud as he could up river.

"Somebody call the cops and an ambulance right now, there's one of them lost! Probably drowned," some teen yelled to the others. There must have been at least fifteen teenagers running along the tracks and out to the river's bank. Everyone was yelling Rink's name. I saw a cop car with its lights flashing on the Iowa side by the bridge where we began. It appeared someone was talking to the cops.

I collapsed into the mud on my hands and knees and threw up. I couldn't stop gagging and retching. My stomach hurt from the dry heaves. A few feet away Bear was sitting with his knees propped up, holding his head as he cried uncontrollably.

"You fucker, Rink!" Blackie screamed at the river, which just ignored him.

Off in the distance, I heard sirens getting closer. I saw several men jumping out of cars with flashing lights running toward us. I saw cop cars on the Illinois bridge stopping all traffic. Adults lined the safety fence along the roadway of the bridge. They were peering down at all the commotion and looking curiously at us.

"Dispatch. Call Bellevue and stop all river traffic heading north from that dam and also call the Dubuque dam. Tell them we have a possible 315 here at East Dubuque and we'll have search parties starting when they get here. Notify the river police to keep all small craft out of this area. The search team will need all the space they can get," a cop shouted into his radio.

Another cop barked out orders to the teens. "All right, everybody out of here right now. Get in your cars and clear the whole area."

Cars were turning in every direction to head out of the parking lot. More sirens could be heard as well as a helicopter coming from the Dubuque airport. There was some type of deep blast from a horn I'd never heard before. It was an unusual looking boat with all kinds of equipment and men on board. They were talking back and forth with a cop on the radios and the cop pointed towards the railroad bridge.

Sand was stuck to the left side of Bear's face where he had flung himself on the beach, bawling like a banshee. Blackie tried to take a punch at another cop who was trying to console him. He just kept screaming that the guy was a fucker, and to get the blanket off him. Traffic was again moving across the Illinois bridge and the cold deep river just kept flowing on, after swallowing my friend. It didn't care; water had no emotion. It reminded me of home for an instant.

There were two things I remembered on the way home. One was how itchy that wool blanket was around me. It reminded me of Bushy's whiskers when I'd would kiss his cheek after taking a swig of beer before going to bed. All of us kids were allowed—no, *obligated*—to occasionally stand in line and kiss his cheek and then take a swig of beer from Ma's bottle. The other thing I remember was the cop talking to dispatch.

"No, the four of them jumped off the railroad bridge and one is an apparent 315. They're dredging the channel now. I'm taking each one home. Roger, and out."

I don't remember passing Sunbeam Bakery, Foster Manufacturing, Eagle's Grocery Store, or even hitting the tracks next to St. Peter's Lutheran Church. The smell of hog and cow shit brought me back from my stupor, and we stopped to let Blackie out of the car. I heard him begging for mercy and calling his mother names as she threw him on the dirt yard and whipped him with the strap. I didn't care; I didn't care about anything.

Dad was already home from work and he and ma came to the car to talk to the cop while dozens of kids came running from everywhere. Enraged, Dad ground his teeth, stared through me, and said to get up to bed. I was in a dream state. I don't remember going up the stairs to my bed. I didn't care what kind of beating I was about to receive. I felt nothing. I was numb. I had a wall of self-protection around me that would keep me safe for decades to come, a wall I'd been building all along.

I did not get beaten. Instead, there was total silence. I fell into a deep sleep, deeper than I'd ever experienced and awoke the next morning to see Dad's car was gone. He'd left for work like it was an ordinary day, like nothing horrible had happened. Down in the kitchen, Ma was listening to Gordy Kilgore on KDTH radio. I caught the tail end of a story about a nine-year-old boy drowning the day before. She looked up at me with sagging bulldog skin under her eyes, empty bloodshot eyes from another night's drinking binge. She screwed the top on the near empty bottle of Jim Beam and placed it next to full bottles of Squirt pop. I noticed a full Jim Beam bottle there as well, all of which spelled trouble with a capital T. None of my brothers and sisters were home, as was our custom. As soon as we could, each of us would leave for the day and go our own ways. It was safer outside than it was in.

"You are are not to go out of the yard until further notice. Do you understand?" she screamed.

"Did they find Rink?" I asked.

"Did you hear me? Are you listening? Do you want me to tell your father when he gets home? Do not leave this yard," she snapped.

"Yes, I understand. Did they find Rink?" I asked again.

She turned and began coughing and hacking as she lit another cigarette. With a deep breath, she blew some smoke rings toward the refrigerator and said nothing more to me. I let the screen door slam against its frame and went to the picnic table, which was sitting on a smooth patch of cement.

I picked a branch off of the purple lilac tree a few feet away. This was her favorite weapon of choice when we misbehaved. The whipping motion could quickly tear the skin as it popped in the air like Roy Roger's whip when he was moving cattle. I pulled at the bark with my fingernails until I was able to expose the slippery underside of the thin whip. I tied the pieces of bark into rings like the smoke rings she'd blown against the refrigerator moments earlier. I watched a pile of ants eating a dead fish fly in the seam of the cement. Even though it was long dead, I felt sorry for it to be gobbled up like that. I took the stick and started swatting at the pile and they scattered in all directions. I thought of Rink.

Day after day the same routine was repeated. I was never cussed at or hit. I did not have to stand at attention in the corner for hours as in the past. I was never shoved and had no work boots thrown at my back. I was ignored: not a word was said to me by either parent. That treatment was strange and it was uncomfortable. I would much rather have been beaten than to be grounded and stuck with Ma all day.

It was a Tuesday. That was the day Fritz smoked his fish at the back of his yard. I saw him walk down the path past the bent wire fence. He waved, but I just turned my back and continued scratching the cement with another lilac branch.

I heard the phone ring from inside. "Where'd they find him?" I heard Ma say into the phone through the open window.

I walked to the door but did not enter. "No, the news was on last night but I had a few too many to remember. When did they find him? When is the funeral? I suppose the wake will be at Humphrey's, being as he was Catholic," she continued. "Okay, thanks for calling."

I heard another beer bottle open and the chair scraped heavily across the linoleum as she sat down. I could see smoke coming out the open window and heard the TV playing *As the World Turns*. She said nothing to me. I walked the thirty feet to the end of the backyard near the rhubarb plant alongside the garage. The cool grass was a temporary diversion as I lay down. I stared at the plant's root system and pulled at the large leaves and focused on the reddish hue. It took every bit of energy I could to do even that.

It had been six days since the only words spoken to me were about being grounded. At supper that night the silence ended. "Mac's coming tomorrow night with Bear and taking the two of you to Humphrey's Funeral Home," Ma announced as if this was something people did at night. "Rink was found directly beneath the railroad bridge, stuck in a tree at the bottom of the river. He either broke something and drowned or just drowned from being stuck down there. Either way, the kid's dead," she said as ashes from her cigarette fell onto her plate.

Bushy didn't say a word. He chased his food with a gulp of Jim Beam and ate like he'd never eaten before. Not a word was said by any of the seven of us kids. We never talked at the table. That was not allowed.

"Hi, Twink," Mac said the next night as I got into the back seat with Bear. "I want you two fellas to know that we're so glad you're not hurt or dead. And that we are all disappointed in what you kids did. I don't have a clue what was going through your minds to jump off that bridge. I can't imagine what Rink's family must be feeling right now."

"Mac," I said as we headed down East 22nd Street towards Humphrey's Funeral home. "I've never seen a dead person before and don't know what to expect. Will he be sitting up and saying good-bye to us, or what? I'm kind of scared."

"No, son, he will be lying in what is called a casket. It may or may not be open. He'll look like he is sleeping, and his hands will be folded. You two can take my hands when we go look at him if you want."

Bear pressed a fist against his chest. "I feel sort of sick, Dad."

"I've seen plenty of dead people in the War," Mac said consolingly. "This won't be too bad. You guys just stand next to me and I'll help you through it."

When we entered the funeral home, two things immediately slapped me in the face. One was the overwhelming smell of flowers and the other was the silence from so many people gathered together in one place. Mac wrote something in a book by the front door and took our hands. I felt secure and scared at the same time. There were rows of chairs like we had at Sunday school at St. Peter's Lutheran Church, all lined up behind pews, also like at church. People were crammed in the room and I heard some loud crying and some gentle sniffles.

Over to my left, Rink's dad was sitting on a folding chair, bent forward with his head in his hands, his elbows resting on his thighs. He wasn't crying. He was just staring at the floor. Behind him were Rink's brothers. Two of them squinted their eyes at me to say how much they hated my guts probably. Another brother held on to his father's right shoulder, giving his dad support with his rippled arm muscles showing through the button down shirt.

The entire event seemed like a dream. I don't remember seeing Rink's mom. I don't remember who else was there. We stood in line and waited as everyone slowly said his or her good-byes to Rink, and all I could see was a casket ahead. I squeezed Mac's hand, and he said in his usual deep gravelly voice, "It'll be okay, Twink. Nothing will happen to you."

Moments later there he was, and it wasn't as if he was asleep. It didn't even look like him. I did not recognize my friend who a few days earlier was flipping his eyelids inside out and bragging about how well he was doing lifting weights in the back yard with his brothers. His fingernails seemed longer than they should have been. There was a huge black spot on his face that was partially covered with pink make-up like our moms would use whenever they went to the bars for a euchre tournament or to church. His hands were wrinkled and shriveled and the right eye was opened just a little to where I saw some white. His head was larger than normal and seemed like the shape of a watermelon. There were pieces of dented skin or what seemed like holes all over his arms. Gone were his muscles. Gone was his smile. This was not my friend.

Thoughts came with a sickening swirl. *What happened to him? Why wasn't it me? Who was this person? This is not my friend. This is not Rink.*

We didn't speak to anyone. The three of us left after what seemed like a week of being there. Bear began sobbing uncontrollably and Mac released my hand and hugged him. Though I was with people, like always, I was alone. We walked to the parked car, and I felt numb. I didn't cry. I was pissed off.

How the hell could such a strong kid—the strongest of us all— have allowed that to happen? What were his last thoughts? How much did he fight? Why didn't he make it up to the top? A million other questions raced through my mind.

"We're going to Whitey's Tap. I need a boiler maker," Mac said. "You guys can get a pop at the table but you can't sit at the bar."

Moments later we were sitting staring at our glasses of Pepsi, filled more with ice than soda. Mac was at the bar, talking about the wake. Everyone was talking about it. Nearly all the men present had been or were going out of respect for Rink's dad. Many of them had either fought in the War or attended church with the family. Regardless, there was a connection between the men. It was like some kind of bond and in a strange way, they had some connection with me and Bear. Many of them came to our table and asked if we were okay and if they could buy us some chips or candy. We declined their offers.

I saw Bear pushing his glasses up on to the bridge of his nose as he took a sip of Pepsi and set the glass down, not saying a word. I smelled the stale air from years of cigarette smoke and spilled beer that had permeated the walls and floor. I picked at the metal tacks holding the plastic chair together and noticed the grime on the metal legs. It reminded me for a second of Blackie's kitchen. I wondered what he thought about seeing Rink.

Mac slammed his glass down on the bar and ordered another boilermaker. "Who the hell would show a kid like that?" he said, his deep voice sounding angry. All the men lining the bar nodded in agreement.

"I was in Anzio. I was in Normandy, and many other places. I've seen dead people in all ways that a regular person cannot imagine. But to see that little kid like that was not right. Why the hell did they do that?"

A fella down at the end of the bar with a missing arm responded, "Yeah, nearly six days stuck in a tree at the bottom of the river would really cause some damage. I'll bet the catfish and mud loppers chewed him up along with any other critters down that deep."

A second guy said, "I saw shit like that on Omaha Beach, about three days after we pushed ahead off the sand. It's amazing what happens to a body underwater. But that was salt water. Who knows what chewed on him? And I agree. Why would they show the body like that?"

"What was with his head? Why was it oblong?" one guy asked.

"My nephew on the rescue squad said it might have been from where he hit that tree on impact when he jumped. Who knows? They should never have had an open casket," another responded.

The middle-aged bartender gave Mac his drink. "Well, thank your lucky stars it wasn't your kids over there that died."

He patted the top of my head. "Yeah, that's right," he said. "But this one's not mine. He might as well be, though. He's always at our house and I threaten to claim him on my taxes each year. The one with the glasses is my son. Both are good kids and having a rough time right now. Call it fate or luck, I am so thankful neither of them was hurt, or worse."

Chapter Fifteen: Saved

"Twink! Hey, Twink!" came the sound of Bear's voice as I sat there staring at the fire escape from under the elm tree at Audubon School; the elm tree, almost a sacred place and my refuge that day.

"I went to your brother's house, and he said he dropped you off here in the old neighborhood after the graveside service," Bear said. "I figured you might be around the school somewhere."

For a moment I didn't know where I was or how much time had passed since I'd said good-bye to my dad at the cemetery. I must have been there quite awhile as my shirt was sweat-dampened, and my pants were wrinkled from sitting up against the elm. It was comforting to see my boyhood friend.

He pushed his glasses up the bridge of his nose, like always. Like nothing had changed in his world. "What are you doing? How are you feeling?" He squinted down at me, his face full of concern. "Do ya want to go get some coffee or something to eat? Is there anything I can do?"

"Awe, I've just been here thinking about the past and how much life sucks sometimes. Yeah, it'd be great to go somewhere and talk. Things won't get any easier just sitting here, beating myself up," I said.

A few minutes later, we were seated at a nearby restaurant. A waitress appeared, chewing on a small cud of gum, paper and pen ready for action. "What'll youse two gents have?"

"I'll just have a cheeseburger, fries, and Pepsi," I told her as Bear ordered the same.

Bear removed his glasses, and rubbed his eyes. "Jesus, can you believe all the people there at St. Peter's for your dad? He had lots of friends from the looks of it."

"I don't remember anybody who was there," I said, avoiding his yes. "All I remember is how he looked better in the casket than in life, fighting cancer. God, what a shame; he was such a fighter and gave his all."

"I know how you feel. I remember when Dad passed. I was there at his bedside with Ma at the hospital when he died," Bear said softly. "Worst feeling ever."

Staring at the table with no energy to raise my head, I nodded in agreement. "Yep, Mac was the best. And ya know, for the last ten years of his life, my Dad tried to be civil after he quit drinking. That's the shame of it. He actually *was* a different person. He would call me in Florida to talk and always asked how I was doing and his concern was genuine." My throat ached at the memory. "Why, there were times when he even gave me advice on dealing with people. I still remember how he hated my guts growing up, but I also remember these past ten years when we finally got along."

"Yeah," Bear said, his eyes widening. "If it wasn't for your old man, I wouldn't be sitting here right now. Jesus, it seems like yesterday when he pulled me from my car just before it exploded when that train hit it."

Many years earlier, Bear hadn't seen the train coming and the guard arms didn't work to prevent him from driving onto the railroad tracks. He was crossing at the corner of East 22nd and Kniest Street when that train slammed into his car just behind the driver's seat. The car, not Bear, was cut in half. I was in Bear's house, watching TV with Mac, and we heard the ungodly crash. First, there was a constant blowing of the horn, like tug boats waiting for the lock to open. Then came the smash. A ceramic angel placed on top of the television set rattled and fell to the floor, breaking into a million pieces. The dishes in the cabinet rattled, and a cup was dislodged from its saucer. I felt the impact of the crash in my chest, a deep vibrating rumble.

Mac and I jumped up to see what happened a mere fifty feet away on the tracks. We were there at the heavy wooden front door in time to see Bear and his car being shoved down the rails. It was like slow motion photography, it was happening and we couldn't stop it. I couldn't run fast enough to get to him. And Mac? Lord, his scream was louder than the train. His son, and my best friend, was being rammed helplessly toward St. Peters Church. I shuddered at what could have been a disaster.

The back half of the car was snagged into the massive train wheels, wheels still moving but trying desperately to stop; the horn kept blowing, the sound of it filling the air with a sort of wailing. Sparks from the collision tried to ignite the dry, dead grass along the railroad bed. The bumper of his car hit a telephone pole and twisted like a piece of warm licorice. There was shattered glass everywhere. The dislodged back half of the car was moving slower because of the friction as it dug deeper into the dirt every twenty yards or so. School papers flew into the air like a tornado had ripped open a school. I remember Bear clinging to the steering wheel like he was still in control and trying to drive ahead of the engine. Little did I know he had been knocked unconscious.

Back about one hundred yards, the first of the boxcars derailed and slid on its side, slamming into a car stopped at the crossing and flattening the engine and hood of the car. Some people were running for safety and others were running into the danger, wanting to have a closer look. Down the tracks there was a kid who, a moment earlier had been trying to cross ahead of the train. He threw his bike down onto the tracks, took off running towards the dirt backyards, and jumped a fence for safety. Bear's car tried to miss it, but couldn't. The bike was now being rammed down the tracks by half of a Chevelle that was being pushed by a locomotive. One boxcar, way back up the tracks, knocked down a telephone pole, sparks were coming from the wires, and flames were shooting from under Bear's car. It looked hopeless, completely hopeless.

My dad . . . who was now in another world, but who in this one, was surely in the right place and the right time at that moment, was stopped at the next crossing, waiting in his car. When the impact occurred, he jumped out and ran towards Bear who had been pushed down the tracks. He was ahead of Mac and me by several yards. His limp was not evident, which I didn't think about at the time. He grabbed Bear under the armpits and with all his strength, yanked him to safety onto the grassy bank, away from the gravel bed of the rails. By the time Mac and I caught up, Dad was already giving Bear mouth-to-mouth breaths and chest compression CPR, and he kept yelling out to anyone, *someone,* to call for help.

I remember running faster than I'd ever run in my life to 2126 Kniest Street. I took the steps four at a time, pushing off the opened door, jerked the yellow wall phone from its perch in the kitchen and called the cops, screaming and trying to be coherent, begging for help. I was still on the phone when I felt the rumble inside the house and heard the explosion. It was Bear's Chevy Chevelle gas tank blowing up.

I leapt to the sidewalk from the porch and in a second was at my Dad's side. He was still working on Bear. People were showing up in droves and everyone was standing in a circle looking down at my dad and Bear. The fire from the explosion wasn't even noticed by us with much concern, as it was some fifty yards up the tracks. I heard sirens coming closer and smelled the oil along the rails and heard the engine of the train still running. Everyone was coming. Everyone.

"Come on son! Come back to us! Don't go away," Mac was crying as he yelled towards Bear.

'Come on, Dad. Bring him back to me. Help will be here soon!' I thought in panic.

And he did come back! Bear returned to the land of the living, coughing and spluttering, wiping his eyes. The best part of Bushy was present that day. My dad saved my best friend. Bear was out of the hospital in a few days. I remember Mac hugging Bushy and thanking him over and over. I didn't know they even knew each other. The *Telegraph Herald* wanted to do a story of a local hometown hero, but Bushy refused. He said later he did what anyone else would have done.

"Here's your food, fellas," the waitress said as she set the plates down. "Youse guys want more Pepsi?"

I looked up at her, hoped she had someone good waiting for her at home. "Yes, I do, and I'll have some black coffee also."

"You dad was like an angel out of nowhere that day," Bear said. "I'll never forget him and what he did for me. But I'll also never forget what he did to you."

We commenced to eating, heads lowered. Some guy stopped by the table and clapped Bear on the shoulder. "Bear, how the hell are youse doing? Why are youse all dressed up? I never seen you wearing a tie before."

Bear looked down at his tie, like he was surprised to see it. "I was at the funeral for Bushy Kramer. This is his son, we call him Krame. He and I have been best friends for years. Grew up together."

"Well, it's a small world," the guy said as he stuck out his hand to shake mine. "I'm Jason Kuberitz. My dad worked with your dad for years at Mazewood, and then when Celotex bought it out. He was at the funeral today along with about twenty of the others from the old plant. I never knew him, but he seemed to be well liked."

Jason pulled a chair from the table and joined us, without asking permission, which was fine with me. It felt like a day without rules. He told me how he'd heard from his dad how all the guys at the plant liked Bushy. He talked liked he knew him.

"Boy, cancer's a bitch, isn't it? How old was he?" he asked.

"Fifty-three," I said.

"I remember my dad talking about your dad, who could make anything out of metal. My old man was your dad's supervisor for many years and always said how he never missed a day of work, and could zip through about six euchre games after lunch. Whenever the guys would pick on him your dad would always say "Ha ha, very funny.""

He tapped a few beats on the table, his fingers like drumsticks. "That was a standing joke at our house when somebody was picked on. Remember the flood of '65 when your dad was picked up in a small john boat at your front door?"

I nodded and couldn't help but smile. "Sure do. The river came all the way to our front door. I remember dad carrying his black metal lunch pail out to the curb and getting in the middle of the boat."

Jason grinned, and tapped some more. "That was my dad who picked him up. He said of all the people willing to work, Bushy would be the one."

I thought back to that day, remembering it like it was yesterday. The rain had been coming down sideways and the wind was howling something fierce. I was sixteen years old and stood looking out the front window as the boat powered off, with all the occupants hunkered forward for protection.

"Well," Jason said, "I have to run. Sorry about your dad. He made a big impact on others." He shook my hand again and left.

We fell silent for a few minutes, lost in our own thoughts. "Hey, have you been by the old house since you came back?" Bear asked.

"Yeah, I walked past it on the way back from Linwood Cemetery, on my way to Audubon."

Bear's eyes lit up. "Did ya notice the discolored spot where 'Kramer's TV Repair' sign once hung?"

"No, I didn't." The idea of Dad's old sign disappearing socked me in the gut, sort of a final finality. "Isn't that some shit after all these years? Wow, hard to believe. It's kind of sad. There was a guy's dream and goal that he met in life, and is left with only a stain on the side of a house."

Bear cocked his head. "Why'd he do that?"

I told him what I could remember. "He bought some type of home education kit about TV repair and he used to sit up studying night after night out of the four black, three-ring note books. They were full of schematics of all types of televisions, tube designs with numbers on them, capacitors and resistors. He memorized every part of each of them. It seemed it took a few years for him to get it down pat."

"But why did he do it?" Bear asked.

I scratched my head, but it didn't take a genius to figure the obvious. "Looking back, I suppose it was to take care of all of us kids and to be able to afford our vacations."

"Hmm, some of the things I remember about back then were his TV business and how you guys would always go on vacation." Bear crackled and fixed what little hair he had left. "The farthest my family ever went was to go fishing off the little bridge in Dyersville."

I finished my coffee, visualizing those days in my mind's eye. "Dad would always lend our TV out to whomever needed one repaired. Then we'd watch him sit on the floor behind the broken one with a mirror out in front, watching the screen and trying to correct the problem. We'd gather on the floor eating popcorn off newspapers spread out like a picnic blanket. We pretended to watch television. Of course the picture was either running up or down, sideways, or totally gone."

We looked at each other and cracked up laughing. "Then something would crackle and snap. We heard 'son of a bitch' as he got a shock. There were TVs in our living room, on the table out in the kitchen; everywhere you looked sat a television. At times, he'd take my brother Mark with him to hold the mirror for him when he made house calls."

"I'll bet that scared the shit out of Mark didn't it?" Bear asked.

"Oh, no, just the opposite," I said feeling a sudden surge of what felt like joy. "Whenever Bushy would ask one of us for help, it was a time of great pride and excitement as a little kid. Anyway,

Mark did that with him many times and was always happy to go along."

Bear pushed his glasses up. "He had that television business for years didn't he?"

I leaned forward and fiddled with the saucer. "Well, like I said, it was probably because of all of us kids to care for and the fact he liked to travel. He needed the money for our yearly vacations. It seemed like that was the only time he was pleasant. Hearing Jason Kuberitz tell it, Dad liked to go to work. Of all the things he hated in life, his job was the worst. He got up every morning cussing out loud about having to go to work and was really mean at that time of day. If the plant ever called after hours when they needed him to return, we had strict orders to say he was not home."

"What about the other times, your vacations," Bear said, looking so interested I tried not to embellish to make the story better. For once, I was telling the truth, the way it was with my dad.

"Well, as vacation time came around, his mood lightened and you could feel excitement in the air."

"So," Bear said, looking at me directly, "your dad was a master at hiding his feelings like someone else I know, huh?"

I just smiled and Bear continued.

"Jesus, remember the time you guys came home from Yellowstone and there were bear paw marks on the windows and doors of your Dad's car? I remember there were kids that came from all over looking at it. That car was quite the hit."

"Yeah, Dad always wanted to see every state in the country," I said listing mentally the ones he'd missed. "I don't know if he ever did, but that was a goal of his. Holy crap, I remember trips we'd take before the younger ones were born. My sister got the back seat all to herself to sleep and spread out at night and Mark and I each slept on either side of the transmission hump on the floor, all curled up on the black rubber floor mats sprinkled with small rocks and dirt. So we would pull over and dad and ma would sleep in the front seat while the three of us older ones slept in the back. When we woke in the morning Mark and I would poke fun at each other because we had little rocks stuck in our cheeks or the floor mat imprinted on our faces."

"I know every year you guys went somewhere. Did you ever get to see all the states?" Bear asked.

"No. But looking back now, it was quite an experience nobody else in the neighborhood had. I saw the Presidents at Mount Rushmore, Custer's Battlefield and Wall Drugstore. The Corn Palace in Mitchell, South Dakota was our first major stop. It was the second day of our trip. Mark and I each were given five dollars to spend for the week. We blew it all in one aisle. He bought a bow and arrow and I bought a tomahawk. Total cost for each was about four dollars and seventy-five cents. We were broke for the week but boy were we happy. At least until his arrow broke later that day when we stopped for gas. He shot at a potato chip bag in the grass at a Pure gas station somewhere in western South Dakota. The arrow made a loud crack as it hit the air pump. He sat there crying, trying to hold the broken pieces of wood together as if they'd magically mend."

Bear looked interested. "I never knew that."

I laughed at the memory. "Dad came out from paying for the gas and saw what had happened. He turned and went back into the station. Moments later he was walking over to Mark and patting his shoulder and helped him carry the broken arrow and bow. He had a bag in his hand from the last time he went into the station. I felt so sorry for Mark whose tears had dried yet continued to sob. Before dad started the car, he reached around to the back seat and fumbled with the bag. He gave each of us a candy bar. We pulled out, and as we did, I stood on the seat to look out the back window at the untouched potato chip bag and even to this day, I remember thinking 'I guess nothing lasts forever.'"

"What happened to your tomahawk?" Bear asked.

I offered a slight smile. "The head came unglued and fell off two weeks later when Rink and I were trying to kill pigeons at Audubon. Rink's Dad said that's what I deserved for buying Jap shit."

Bear grinned. "That sounds like something he'd say. Where else did you guys go?"

I bit my lip and thought about it. "Lets see . . . we visited the zoo at St. Louis, Mackinaw Island and went over the Mackinaw Bridge and then took a ship from Ludington, Michigan to Milwaukee. I remember seeing the Rockies and Cheyenne, Wyoming. The first limousine I ever saw was in Hot Springs,

Arkansas. I can't remember how often Old Faithful would erupt with its magnificent spray up in the air, but we got to see it."

I was on a roll now and Bear knew it by the way he settled in his seat. "The first leach I ever saw was when Dad picked one off his foot while we were staying at a cabin in Wisconsin on a fishing trip. I was probably nine or ten years old. He sprinkled salt on it and waited for it to curl up in a ball. He then just threw it off on the ground and with his foot still bleeding, continued talking about something from a previous conversation."

Bear looked dubious. "Leaches are gross."

"Dad was like a kid on that trip, happy and fun-filled. He bought fishing gear of all types and a can of worms for bait. Mark and he caught rock bass and blue gills. I just caught grass from the bottom. But it didn't matter as we were like a real family during that week. Ya see, overwhelmingly, Dad was a decent guy when we went on vacations."

Bear cupped an elbow with one hand. "So the shit that happened at home just disappeared when you went on trips?"

"Well, for the most part. You see, we weren't allowed to talk in the back seat and certainly no fighting. If we annoyed him, he'd tell us to lean closer to the front seat and then he would hit us in the face with his fist while he continued driving," I said, like this was an ordinary thing dads did. "Let's see, Yellowstone is about 1,000 miles and the impact of the punch lasted about 250 miles—so I probably got hit only four times out and back," I said laughing.

"I went to the Museum of Science and Industry and the Shedd Aquarium in Chicago on vacation. And Bear, did I tell ever tell you about being lost, and believing I was all alone?"

"No, but this should be good," Bear said, fixing his glasses. "You always have been a magnificent storyteller, and I never knew when you were spreading shit or if it was true."

"No, no shit," I said. "This is a true story. We were at the Science and Industry Museum in Chicago. I was somehow separated from the rest of the family by the coal mine elevator. I was so enamored with how it all worked, I watched for several minutes while the rest of them wandered off to that big heart you could walk through and then on to the fetuses in bottles. I don't know how much time passed, but eventually I was bored and looked around. Nobody was there. I sat on the floor crying, thinking I was lost forever."

The waitress appeared with our checks. "Youse guys alright over here?"

We nodded and I continued my story. "After what seemed like hours, a big black man with a badge came up to me and asked where my parents were. I remember sobbing and telling him I didn't know. The fellow spoke into a mic on his left shoulder. "Headquarters, we have a 1012 by the coal elevator."

"Roger. What's his name?" the dispatcher responded.

Again he spoke into his left shoulder. "All he says is 'Krame' and he's about ten years old or so."

Immediately a voice came over the loud speaker, describing me and where I was.

Within minutes, Dad appeared. "Thanks, sir for helping him."

The guard nodded and turned away. I watched him disappear into the crowd, and from that moment on, I've always had a special place in my heart for black folks. They weren't the bogeymen I'd heard from all the parents in the neighborhood."

Dad looked down at me and scolded me for getting lost. "Stop crying. Men don't cry," he said.

I continued telling Bear more stories about our vacations. "Cincinnati, Memphis, the Smoky Mountains, northern Minnesota, Nebraska, Kansas, and more. Ya know, when you think about it, we had quite the experiences," I rambled.

"Do youse fellas want some more coffee?" the waitress interrupted.

"Yes, please. You might want to bring a full pot," I said.

"Did Mark have it as bad as you?" Bear asked.

"Ya know, we've talked about our past for years and tried to analyze it. There's all kinds of abuse. Not just physical, but mental abuse can be just as bad. I remember Mark telling me that when he went off to college, Dad gave him twenty-five dollars and shook his hand. That was only the second time in his life dad had touched him without hitting him. The first time was when he finished putting together a crib for someone while dad apparently watched. When he finished he hugged Mark across the shoulders and said, 'Good job.'"

"Mark played football, wrestled and ran track in junior high and high school. Just like me, Dad and Ma never came to see him compete," I said, wrestling with my emotions. "They did support his musical talents though."

Bear nodded. "Yeah, he was quite the musician. Didn't he play the violin or something?"

"Oh yeah," I said, drumming my fingers on the table. "Be sure to ask him about that. No, he played the viola, drums and oboe. One time in the tenth grade when Mark got off the Linwood bus in front of Huey's, those thugs Aaron and Brian Kretchmeyer were there smoking cigarettes and hanging around. They gave him shit about being a sissy violin player and Mark called 'em morons and laughed that they didn't even know the difference between a viola and a violin."

"Oh shit!" Bear said. "That was pretty stupid. Those were the two meanest guys in the entire neighborhood. What happened?"

"I remember it like it was yesterday," flipping through the scrapbook of my mind. "We were eating supper when Mark came home and threw his shattered viola case on the living room floor. We heard a thunderous crash as he fired his books across the room. Dad put his beer down and jumped up to see what was happening. I followed close behind. Just as we made it to the living room, Mark was coming down the stairs with a baseball bat." Like good storytellers everywhere, I paused for effect. "He was going out for revenge."

Bear toasted me with his water glass and we both laughed. "Holy shit! Mark did that? He's always so quiet and proper."

"Yeah, just don't push him or you'll see rage like never before."

Bear fiddled with his glasses, finally got them aligned. "Then what happened?"

"Well," I said. "Dad asked Mark what the hell had happened, and Mark explained how he'd gotten off the bus and what was said. The two Kretchmeyers rushed him and he slipped on the ice and snow when he was tackled. The older one punched him in the face while the other moron took his gym bag and scattered stuff all over the place. Then they kicked him and stomped his viola case. Mark was going back, aiming to get even.

Dad asked me what the hell I was doing there, gawking like a curious rooster, and told Mark to go in the kitchen and eat his supper.

"Without saying a word dad left the house, and slammed the door behind him. It wasn't ten minutes later when we heard the front door open and Mark and I ran into the living room. Dad was leading, followed by the two Kretchmeyers, Aaron and Brian. In a voice that could crack a cement block, he turned to them and said, 'Sit!'"

"He held up his massive hands like he'd use 'em if he had to. 'I've killed men with these two hands when I was in the army,' he shouted. 'If you ever go two on one again, you'll answer to me! Now, get out of here.'"

Although I'm sure Bear knew the answer, he had to ask. Otherwise, my story wouldn't be complete. "Did they ever bother any of you again, especially Mark?"

"Nope," I said, as I smiled and stirred my coffee.

There was a moment or two of quiet as we each fixed our brew to our liking. I just stirred the brown liquid around in a circle for quite some time, absorbing the quiet and feeling alone, even though I was sitting with my lifelong friend. Isn't that how it goes? When two people are as connected as Bear and I have always been, you just know when to speak and when to listen.

After a few minutes Bear asked, "Hey, do ya want to go up to Eagle Point Park?"

"Yeah. That'd be nice," I said, my heart filling with memories spilling over like the coffee onto the cheap table. "That'd be real nice."

Chapter Sixteen: Good Times

Not much was said as we drove back through the neighborhood. I felt the muffled bump as we crossed the railroad tracks covered with hog and cow shit and again saw the old house I'd left years before. As Bear stopped at the stop sign, I turned and looked out the back window and saw the imprint on the house Bear had mentioned, the empty space where the TV repair sign once hung.

We passed Bethany Home where I'd once come to a screeching halt on a stolen bicycle from Municipal Pool and dropped it in the gutter while several old folks sat on the porch. We turned up onto Rhomberg Avenue and crossed over to Garfield where I saw trains sitting, waiting for their loads to head north towards Minnesota, down the steep bank I remembered where we jumped off the train on the way to the pool. Ahead was the lumberyard where we stole the plank for our adventure at Flat Rock.

'God, nothing has changed,' I thought.

Neither of us spoke a word, and it was fine with me. Turning onto Shiras Avenue, I wondered if Eagle Point was still the same. The CCC had built Eagle Point Park during the depression. It was, and remains a landmark for Dubuquers and will be for generations to come. There were pavilions built of hand-laid limestone, a winding paved road that led through tree-lined rest areas. The road was dotted with picnic tables and restrooms, created from backbreaking labor all those years before. Modern times led to the installation of tennis courts and a water fountain where small children once cooled their tiny bodies and now those same people, all grown up and parents themselves, had brought their children to repeat history. And on and on it goes.

Bear pulled into the overlook with the dam visible below. The area had several benches and was protected by a chain link fence, similar to our neighbor, Fritz. A hundred feet or more below was the dam and the Wisconsin Bridge spanning over the Mississippi. Down to our right was the railroad bridge connecting Iowa to Illinois and below that was the car bridge going into Illinois. We could see all of it from our vantage point.

"Can ya see Flat Rock over by the lock and dam?" Bear asked.

"Yeah," I said, shielding my eyes from the sun. "That was such a great day wasn't it?"

Bear shook his head in amazement. "And you, ya crazy son of a bitch, coming up with the plan to hop that train and then steal the diving board. Jesus, we were lucky we didn't get caught."

"Ya know, that river brought us many good times and an equal number of bad times. God, we're so lucky it wasn't us stuck in that tree." I gazed off in the distance. "What a bunch of stupid assholes we were."

We sat there a while longer, I guess mulling over the truth of my statement. "What ever happened to Rink's family?"

Bear leaned forward and rubbed his hands together. "I figured you heard. Living in the South, I suppose you're like a million miles away. His two older brothers were killed in Viet Nam. I heard his dad started drinking, quit the church, and ended up killing himself years ago. He shot himself in the head with a rifle he took off a dead Jap during the War."

"Damn," I said. "Life sucks."

Bear just stared at me for a moment and looked away. Silence overtook us, until Bear spoke. "Hey, let me ask ya. When was the last time you saw Blackie?"

"Kind of funny. It was the day Rink died and the cop dropped him off at his house. God, his mother was beating the living shit out of him in that dirt yard! That was the last I saw him. We never played together again. He went on to Catholic school and our paths never really crossed. Oh, I saw him a few times across Audubon playground, but that was it," I said.

"Could ya believe it when he killed himself?" Bear asked.

"Poor fella. Never had a chance," I said, staring down at the dam below.

"You never were big on fishing were ya?" Bear asked out of the blue.

"No, not me. Mark was and still is a fanatic on it."

"I don't even know how. Did you ever fish?" he asked.

"Yeah. Just not there, in the river."

"Dad always had wild hairs where he would come up with new ideas and get into them, one hundred percent. I'm sorta like that now, as an adult, myself," I told him with a smile. "I don't care if it was fishing, golf, railroad model trains, or what. He'd get this wild hair and attack, full steam ahead. Whatever it was, he would research by reading, and then after analyzing the whole thing, he'd move ahead."

Bear rubbed his forehead. "Jesus, remember how Blackie'd always rib you about analyzing everything? Do ya suppose that's where you got that from, your Dad?"

I fidgeted on the hard bench. "I don't know. I think back on those days when we were younger, it was more the fact of *not* getting caught. It might be though." I let out a belly laugh; I couldn't help it. "Wouldn't that be ironic? What if I was that way because of my Dad and yet it was because I didn't want to get caught by my Dad?" I poked a stick in the dirt as I had years before in the backyard with the lilac switch, stirring up ants.

I turned to Bear. "It was at Swiss Valley Park where we first went fishing. Have you ever been there?"

"Jesus," Bear said, punching my left shoulder. "You need to get checked for dementia when you get back to Florida. Don't you remember when we went there and camped for a jamboree with Boy Scouts?"

"Oh yeah, I forgot," I said, and smacked my forehead.

Bear moved closer. "How the hell can you forget the great fart off? God, you had the worst farts of all of us. I remember when it was so cold and there was you, me, and Cliff Beranger in the same tent. You cut one loose and we had to stick our heads out the front tent flap, we gagged so hard. And you? You bastard; you were inside laughing! The scoutmaster yelled at us and told us to go to sleep. Said he didn't want to hear another peep outta us."

"Yeah, too bad we didn't have a match back then. Probably would have blown up the tent, and then some," I said with a smile. "It might have even blown up your socks."

Bear cracked up laughing. "Yeah, god, that was great, wasn't it?"

I took a calming breath. "Anyway, that was where I first fished. No fish at all! Just crawdads. I remember when Dad got this wild hair-brain idea of all of us fishing and we went to Walsh's on a Friday night. I can still remember the uneven, wooden floors that squeaked with every step, regardless of the size of the person or their body weight."

I closed my eyes and saw it all clearly. "They had two aisles of nothing but fishing gear. He'd just paid for two TV jobs and had some cash to spend. We bought several poles, red and white bobbers with those little 'j' shaped clamps that held the line, teardropped sinkers, hooks of all sizes that came in plastic bags, three single-shelved tackle boxes made of grey plastic, and one triple-shelved box made of metal for him, along with pliers, a net for the big ones we caught, and even a small baseball bat to smack to death any giants we might have caught."

"How the hell can you remember all that?" Bear asked.

"Jesus, I'm not shitting you! All us kids got was two and three-inch crawdads. Mark caught the most, down by where the road crossed the stream and the water was maybe three feet deep. I remember Dad never opened his tackle box. He was just there having a drink with Ma and watched us. You know, we never did use that bat," I said, laughing out loud.

Bear still looked interested, so I went on. "I suppose one positive thing that came from that is Mark's always been an avid fisherman. I wonder if he remembers those days at Swiss Valley like I do? Did I ever tell ya, Bear, that my brother is one of the closest people inside my heart? That is, after you." My eyes filled with the thought of it. "He and I have been through so much."

"That doesn't surprise me about your brother. You two went through some bad times together back when we were all young. When did it all end? You know, the beatings and bad times with your dad?" Bear asked.

"I was in eleventh grade and was grounded for being late one night. It was in April or May—I can't remember. I do know it was in 1966," I said, talking fast. "I left the house despite his threat of punishment. I was on the track team and we ran at the Drake Relays in Des Moines. God, what a great day that was. We won the 880- and 440-yard relays and set a record in the 440-yard relay that still stands to this day. I was the fastest and anchored both."

I continued, my body running on adrenaline like the event had just happened. "We won second place in the mile medley relay and I personally won second in the 100-yard dash. And I tell you what, Bear! We were competing against *everyone* in Iowa! I was so pumped up and knew I was going off to college someday on a track scholarship. I'd get out of the North End and out of my house forever. I would never have to work at the Pack. Never."

Bear, being Bear, fell quiet and allowed me to continue. He was always good like that.

"I remember sitting in the back seat of Coach Glab's station wagon returning back to Dubuque. Everyone was laughing and having a great time. I just kept my face to the window thinking during the entire 200-mile trip that I was going to get beat something fierce when I got home."

"So what happened," Bar asked sarcastically. "As your usual self, you are rambling on when all I asked was, when was the last time you were beaten?"

"I'm getting there, you asshole," I said.

"It was at least nine or so at night when I walked into the house. I was surprised to see they'd moved furniture around to where the davenport was now facing the front door. I knew I was in trouble, but figured because I was now known as one of the fastest runners in all of Iowa, I would be forgiven. Dad stood up when I opened the front door, and I tried to show him the many medals I'd won at one of the most prestigious track meets in America. But he didn't want to hear or see anything, and he absolutely would not listen. He ripped his belt from the loops of his brown pants and began swinging at me with the buckle end. I fell to the floor for protection and assumed the usual fetal position. I screamed in pain and saw the blue ribbon from the 440 hooked on to its round metal base, being splattered with blood from my upper back. It was inches from my face, which was now embedded in the stink-filled carpet.

'*How can this be?*' I remembered asking myself, while mentally escaping the pain. '*A few hours ago I was being cheered by people I didn't even know and now I am being pulverized by my dad. It doesn't matter, because it doesn't hurt anymore. Nothing hurts and nothing really matters anymore.*'"

"Krame," Bear said. "C'mon, you're killing me here."

"No, I have to tell you. When you're beaten so much, Bear, there comes a time when you can actually endure the pain and go through the motions of screaming and crying. The whole time it really did not hurt. I figured the more I yelled the sooner he'd quit, since it seemed from my experience that his only reason in doing it was to make me hurt." I glanced at Bear who was looking at the ground. "Beatings were always better than being grounded."

"Holy, crap!" Bear exclaimed. "Why didn't you just run out the door and come to us? You know Mac would have protected you."

"Sometimes, shit just doesn't matter. I know you guys were all there for me. I know Mac would have helped me, but as with many things in Life, I learned early I have only me to protect myself. I learned that in the dark stairwell in the basement at age eight and it still stands to this day. Sort of like those poor POWs from WW II and those guys our age who were tortured in Viet Nam. Anyway, that was the very end of it all. He never touched me again," I said, ending the conversation with a blatant lie. "And it's okay. It's all okay."

Bear pushed his glasses up his nose. "What happened to the case my granddad made for all your track medals?"

"Ya know, I don't have a clue. Somewhere over the years I lost all that stuff. Isn't that something how you, your sisters, parents and even your grandparents all helped me out and had an impact on where I am today? I guess Mac should have taken me off on his taxes after all," I said and we both grinned at the old joke.

"That was so awesome you had a track scholarship for college and then went off to graduate school, and became a physical therapist," Bear said, breaking into applause. "I'm real proud of you for making your dream come true."

My face flushed with emotion. "Thanks Bear, that means a lot. Yeah, I've been lucky with coaches who helped keep me on the straight and narrow and for being gifted with a few brains added in for good measure," I said, speaking not only to my best childhood pal friend sitting there beside me, but to the world itself; the wonderment of it all. "Who would have thought, years ago now, that I'd be the administrator of a large out-patient clinic in Florida and a national public speaker?"

Below we heard the blow of the foghorn from the tug pushing a five-line barge north towards Minnesota. It was stopped, waiting for the lock to open, and then eventually to pass through. Bear and I locked in on the activity a hundred feet below the fence like it was our first time seeing such a sight. My thoughts were interrupted by the sound of an airplane overhead and I looked east towards Wisconsin.

A small commuter plane was banking over the Mississippi, steadying itself toward the Dubuque airport, miles to the south. My thoughts raced back to a couple weeks prior, when Dad was still alive but dying at University Hospital in Iowa City. I was on the same type of plane coming home to say good-bye. It was the last time I saw him alive and the second time in my entire life he'd said, in so many words, that he loved me. That was when I left his room at the hospital, at that precise moment.

It had been a long day.

Chapter Seventeen: Wrong Number

I clipped the end off another Arturo Fuente cigar and sat next to Bear. I was halfway through when Bear asked me something no one ever asked before.

"If you don't want to tell me, it's okay, but why do you suppose he treated you and your brothers so bad? Any ideas?"

"No, it's good to have a friend I can talk to about the past," I told him. "Who really knows why any of us do what we do? I can tell you what *I* feel, but there's no way to explain behavior, to get into someone else's head. There's part of me that wants to think . . . that does think, that there was something that happened to him that he was passing on to us. That . . . I don't know, extenuating circumstances that could explain why he unleashed his demons on my brothers and me. It was right after my last beating when I came home from the Drake Relays. It was just before the Prom. I answered the phone and I remember it like it just happened. As always, I said 'Kramer's' as I spoke into the phone."

"I heard the voice at the other end say, 'Is Krame there?' And then I said, 'Yes, this is he.'"

"The voice said, 'This is your dad.' I didn't recognize the voice, and I told him he had the wrong number, and he hung up. But before I took two steps, it rang again. The guy tells me not to hang up, that his name is Dick Slauserman, and that he's my father. And then it hits me."

"What hit you?" Bear asked quietly.

"I was adopted. *'You are not mine, and that is why I like doing this to you!'* That's what he'd said to me, my dad, eight years earlier. I heard him say it then, that awful day, but how was I supposed to know what it meant? Of course," I said, shaking my head. "I was adopted. God, I was pissed at the world. I was pissed off at the entire universe."

"Whoa," Bear said. "I remember a long time ago you told me you'd met your real dad but you never told me what you meant."

"Yeah, I met him a couple nights later. Dick. Between the night he called, and the time we got together, I was working on processing the realization that *I was adopted*. I realized I'd been beaten by an *outsider* all this time. You remember the bells at

Sacred Heart? That's what it was like—this new information went through me like the feeling of hearing the bells ring. It was overwhelming. I finally knew what he meant—my dad, I mean—when he'd shoved his finger into my chest and told me, '*You are not mine.*' I can still feel on my chest where he jammed his finger into me."

"Jesus, what about your brother and sister? Did they know? What the hell! This doesn't make any sense. And now *I'm* pissed," Bear said as he left the picnic table and went over and kicked the fence.

"Bear, this whole thing is so screwed up. I don't even know where to begin. Ya can't make this shit up."

"Yes, my brother and sister knew about this guy named Dick. Since I was little, I always received a Christmas gift from someone named Dick. I was told to just open it and be quiet. So I did and never asked and never gave it a thought. Here, all those years he'd send me a Christmas present, and I never knew Ma had been married before. I do remember vaguely when I must have been about three or so, running into the kitchen and somebody asking if I wanted my name changed. Little did I know how that would affect my entire life."

"Holy crap!" he exclaimed.

"So anyway, I found out I was of German descent, and this guy, Dick, came and picked me up in *Großpapa's* Volkswagen and took me to my grandparent's home for dinner. It was there I learned Dick was a Lutheran minister, graduate of the University of Chicago, and a former missionary who worked in Africa. At that time he was living in the Northeast and was Editor-in-Chief of the Research Institute of America. Not only that, but he had lots of political ties with the CIA and famous politicians. I was impressed as hell; I mean, think about it! He'd been a quarterback at the same high school I went to later, and was an all-around athlete."

"Holy shit. That's probably where you got your speed."

I smiled at the memory. "He dropped me off hours later at home and gave me $50 for the prom. He said we would forever be in touch. We shook hands and I left the car, pissed at Dad for all the abuse. That was twenty-one years ago, and I have never heard from Dick since."

Bear was gripping the fence, practically bending the top of it with his white knuckles, like I had done years earlier to Fritz's fence. He was crying, tears running down his cheeks. It was my turn to console. It didn't do much good as both of us began sobbing. Using my left arm, I reached across his upper back and squeezed his left shoulder, holding him close. Nothing was said for a long time. We each moved in different directions. He went to the overlook and I walked down to the pavilion and sat by myself for many moments.

Then an emotion-filled Bear started rambling. "Shit Twink! I had no idea. How have you lived with this? Who else knows about this? Damn, I am so pissed. How the hell could people be like that?"

I blew one last smoke ring and flipped the Fuente away. "I don't know. Ya know what though? It's okay," I said. "I feel like I have a grasp on the whole deal. Remember how Ma wouldn't let me play with Tom Wagner because his mother was divorced? She said his mother was white trash. To this day, and as long as I live, I will never forgive her for condemning that lady, and here Ma was the same. What a hypocritical bitch she was!"

"Another thing I have thought about, Bear, was dad being just nineteen years old, and marrying a woman ten years older and there he was, saddled with three kids and an immediate built-in family. Why, he was just eight years older than my sister when he married Ma. He never missed a day at his job which he hated his entire life. If he wasn't working, he was reading or fixing things. I wondered over the years if he was compelled to succeed. I remember one year he brought home boxes full of some type of scrap metal shavings. He used a magnet to separate the pieces, collecting the copper. This went on every night for months, and he used the money to pay for one of our vacations."

Bear had calmed down, but remained silent, the muscles in his jaw clenching with anger.

"Bear, I had no love for Ma, and never will. I blame her more than dad for all that happened to us. She'd bitch if ya hung her with a new rope," I said, as Bear snickered and readjusted his glasses.

"Nothing was ever good enough for her. Nothing was ever pleasant. We were a thorn in her side and never did a day go by without threats of, 'Wait till your dad gets home. You're gonna get it then!'"

"And the cycle went on day after day. Dad walked into the house from a job he hated, into a situation where immediately he heard nothing but complaints and bitching. It was almost always about us boys. I probably would have done the same as he did. Off came the belt, the shoving, or the kicking. I wondered if he did that to us to shut her up. Some days he was exhausted and seemed to have no energy to physically abuse us. He'd take a nap, but before he did, my older brother and the brother beneath me in age had to assume the position (as he liked to call it). While he napped, we were forced to stand two feet away from the corners in the bedroom with our arms at our sides. We had to lean forward so our noses touched the corners. The two walls cupped our heads and that was our only means of support. There we were, for forty-five minutes, to sometimes well over an hour. I eventually grew accustomed to the position and told myself it was strengthening my back."

"Jesus, if that shit happened now, somebody would be going to jail," Bear said in disgust.

"Yeah, but that was in the mid-1950s. It was acceptable, and no matter what, nothing was ever to be said outside of the house about what happened."

"Oh yeah," I continued, "One time Mark twisted his head on the wall to see if dad was asleep. He was not. A second later I heard the heavy weighted thud of dad's work boot hit my brother square in the back. Dad reached down and flung it all the way across the room, hitting Mark square between the shoulder blades. I heard the gasping and whimpering, and then the old standard line came out, the sound of Dad's snarling voice."

"Quit crying, or I'll give you something to cry about!"

"I enjoyed the cool temperature and roughened texture of the plaster board, cradling me that day. I was glad I never turned around. It was several weeks later before Mark could swing a bat on the playground. He used to just sit by the elm tree and watch us play and I saw the difficulty he had standing up off of the roots when the game was over," I said.

Bear winced. "Do you suppose he broke a rib or something?"

"I imagine so," I replied. "I do remember him going fishing day after day at the slew, down by the dump, trying to catch carp.

He always went alone. I have asked myself a million times if that was his safe zone. If that was where he felt a sense of calm. We will never know," I said, staring off into space.

"That person we buried today is my dad and always be. That person, Dick is nothing!" I said emphatically. I continued, Dad is 'Dad' and he was and always will be.

Chapter Eighteen: No More

"You know how all of my six brothers and sisters are so spread out in age, with the oldest being at least nineteen years or so older than the youngest? Well, in a family like that, we didn't even know one another. The younger ones had no idea what us older kids went through. Now here's some incredible shit you will not believe!" I said as Bear again was sitting on the picnic table staring at the ground, and focused on my every word.

"Today after the funeral, Ma gave Dad's American flag that was on his casket to my younger brother. He correctly said it should go to the oldest son, and not to him. Can ya believe this shit? My younger brother found out *today* that the three of us older ones were adopted! He didn't have a clue! I assumed he knew. Is this family screwed up, or what, with secrets like that? And I blame Ma! Anyway—he went nuts. Rightly so. I felt so sorry for him and will for the rest of my life. I'm telling ya, Bear, secrets are no damn good! The irony of it all is that it's because of my younger brother that Dad became such a good friend to me."

"Oh, Jesus Christ! I don't even drink and I could use a bottle of straight booze," Bear said angrily. "It's a wonder you guys aren't all screwed up! Do you have another one of those cigars?"

I looked him square in the eyes. "What are ya talking about? You don't smoke anymore."

"I'm not shitting ya. I want one, if you have an extra. Your stories are killing me!" He held out his hand. "So do ya have one or not?"

I laughed as I went to his car and grabbed another two stogies out of my breast pocket. I clipped and lit the end for him as he choked and gagged while trying to get it burning.

"Remember when Mac caught you smoking and made you go to the garage out back and inhale several times on a cigar and you threw up?"

But Bear was silent again. He couldn't speak, as his thirty-year smoke-free lungs bellowed and heaved while I hit him on the back. I clamped down on my cigar as hard as I could, dropping hot ashes on my pants and giggling about him being a big weenie.

"Screw you," I think he said, through the coughing while I belly-laughed and blew a couple good rings at his face and watched him gag some more.

"Jesus, I think I'll go back to drinking," he said as he threw a perfectly good cigar over the bluff, toward the dam below.

He spit a great hocker on the fence. "So how did your younger brother change everything?"

"Well, here's how I see it. The five older ones all did whatever we could to get out of the house. My sister married young, as did I. And ya know mine failed. My older brother, who's also an overachiever, went his way. The brother two down from me, married at sixteen and was an alcoholic in nothing flat. Now the brother directly beneath me ran away and joined the Marines," I started, while Bear was locked into my story with eyes and ears.

"Remember how every night Dad would drink a bottle of Jim Beam, watching TV in the kitchen, while Ma drank a case of beer in the living room?" I asked him.

"Yeah. I remember you telling me that years ago and that was why you were afraid to go home, because you never knew what would happen."

"Anyway, my brother came home from boot camp, probably looking for a fight. He went to the kitchen where Dad was watching his TV. He apparently pointed at the Jim Beam bottle and said with an antagonistic tone, 'That is exactly why this family is shit. That is why everyone is gone and will never come back!'"

"As I heard years later, Dad got up with tears in his eyes and took the booze bottle and poured it down the drain. He then took the remains of the beer bottles in their case, opened the back door, and threw the case and all out onto the cement that once entombed me below in that black stairwell."

"He went to the living room, pointed at Ma and said, "It all stops now! No more! No more drinking! Do you understand? We've lost our family, and there will be no more of this shit. Tell me you understand!'"

"Wow!" Bear said. "Do you think that's true?"

"Oh yeah," I said. "Dad told me years later how and why he quit drinking. It was all because of my younger brother." I choked on my cigar smoke, just thinking about it.

Bear coughed, coughed again. "Jesus, did they ever go to AA or anything?"

"Too funny! You stupid asshole! Can you see Bushy ever going to a group, standing up and admitting he was wrong, and an alcoholic?"

"Nah, probably not," Bear said. "How'd he change?"

"Bear, this is the best part of all. Only during the last ten years did I realize that he had a heart of gold. He was so intelligent and so caring when the wall came down from the drinking. He read every book out there on positive thinking and self-improvement. He became an artist with watercolors. His voice changed, his demeanor changed, and he was just such a good person. We carried on conversations about an array of topics. We talked for hours at times. His heart and his arms opened up to everyone."

I continued, "As each of us felt it was safe to return home we eventually felt at ease sitting with him out at the picnic table in the back yard and talking. I once asked him why he was so strict with us older ones and not the little ones. He told me he ran out of energy and after putting down the booze, he also realized he could have done better raising us."

Bear smiled. "So he did apologize after all!"

"Well, that was good enough for me," I said. "I'll never forget and never understand why he did all that stuff to me. Neither of them gets a 'pass' and total forgiveness. Ma was never there for us emotionally and caused unbridled pain inside while Dad's contribution was both physical and emotional. But now, I have a good grasp on my life."

"Another neat thing he did was he taught himself to paint in watercolors. His work is pretty impressive. However, he refused to put his name on any of his works as he said they weren't good enough. He put all new lighting in the basement and created his own little studio down there where he would sit alone and do his art. Once when I went home, he invited me down to see what he was working on. I have to tell you, that was the first time in my life I went to the cellar with Dad and wasn't afraid of what was about to happen."

"I'll bet that was an eerie feeling," Bear said.

"I couldn't believe what he had done down there. He installed surround sound and listened to classical music as he painted. He had an easel set up with an incredible painting of a red sled leaning against a snow-lined barbed wire fence with a farmhouse off in the distance and a pheasant flying out of the cornfield. I'm telling you, this guy had talent. He appeared to be full of inner peace. That's what I mean when I think of what a shame it was for him to experience that kind of calm and then get cancer and die," I said.

"Yeah, but just imagine if your brother never started the ball rolling, making him quit drinking, and he never discovered that peace you talk about. Now that would have been a shame," Bear said as I nodded in agreement.

"I have to change the subject for a second because describing what he did to fix up the cellar reminds me of something," Bear said. "When he remodeled the basement, what did he do with the trunk?"

"What trunk? What are you talking about?" I asked, squinting in deep thought.

"Don't you remember in third grade you told me about opening a trunk to go to a secret city?" He laughed and hit me on the arm as if I just lost a game of rock-paper-scissors. "What a crock of crap that was. But I did believe it for quite some time."

"Yea, that was a good one. I figured you'd forget about it and never ask to see it. Aren't imaginations great? That was too funny." I turned to him with all due respect. "Bear, you are without a doubt my closest friend. And I thank you for that. Okay, here's one for ya," I said and started to sing.

After two words out, Bear knew exactly what I was doing and joined me in the chorus.

"Poor Ole Merle, for the Worst is yet to Come—Hey!"

We laughed walking back to the car.

Nobody knows. Nobody's seen. Nobody but me.

###

About the Author

Audubon Elementary School can be seen in the background of this photo of the author at age eight.

David Nelson was the fastest sprinter in Dubuque during his high school years; this earned him a track & field scholarship to attend the University of Dubuque. After graduating he trained as a physical therapist at the University of Iowa. He is retired from that profession, and now wears another hat—he has been named the Cowboy Poet Laureate of Tennessee, and performs his Cowboy Comedy Show nationwide. To book a show or speaking engagement, contact him at david@davidnelsonauthor.com (email) or visit www.davidnelsonauthor.com (web page).

Connect with me online

Twitter: https://twitter.com/authordavidn

Facebook: http://www.facebook.com/DavidNelsonAuthor

Google+: https://plus.google.com/103989658575094708798/

My blog: http://davidnelsonauthor.com/blog

David Nelson's Other Works

PALS: Part One is a memoir of his life until high school graduation. It is a collection of short stories about how he reacted to his experiences with child abuse. It takes the reader into a world where friends helped David cope and survive his formative years.

PALS: Part Two is also a collection of short stories from high school to present day. The reader will see there can be success after child abuse. It is filled with humor, adventure and of course some of the dark side of life.

The Campfire Collection of Cowpoke Poetry is a collection of cowboy poetry and short stories. David in the Cowboy Poet Laureate of Tennessee. He has traveled across America entertaining crowds with his off-beat brand of humor and his unusual insight into life.

Made in the USA
Lexington, KY
31 May 2014